There was silence for such a long time Kennedy wondered if there was a problem with Carl's antique cell phone. Finally, Rose asked, "And so what happens if you get pregnant, and you're too young to actually have a baby?"

Defying all laws of inertia, the acceleration of Kennedy's heart rate crashed to a halt like a car plowing into a brick wall. "What do you mean?"

"Like, what if you're too young but you still get pregnant?"

"How young?" Kennedy spoke both words clearly and slowly, as if rushing might drive the timid voice away for good.

"Like thirteen."

Praise for *Unplanned*
by Alana Terry

"Deals with **one of the most difficult situations a pregnancy center could ever face**. The message is **powerful** and the story-telling **compelling**." ~ William Donovan, *Executive Director Anchorage Community Pregnancy Center*

"Alana Terry does an amazing job tackling a very **sensitive subject from the mother's perspective**." ~ Pamela McDonald, *Director Okanogan CareNet Pregnancy Center*

"**Thought-provoking** and intense ... Shows **different sides of the abortion argument**." ~ Sharee Stover, *Wordy Nerdy*

"Alana has a way of sharing the gospel **without being preachy**." ~ Phyllis Sather, *Purposeful Planning*

D1596729

"Chung-Cha belongs to Christ," Father declared. *"Even if you destroy me, God will still watch over my daughter."*

The agent chuckled.

"And what if I destroy her?"

Praise for *The Beloved Daughter* by Alana Terry

Grace Awards, First Place

IndieFab Finalist, Religious Fiction

Women of Faith Writing Contest, Second Place

Book Club Network Book of the Month, First Place

Reader's Favorite Gold Medal, Christian Fiction

*"...an **engaging plot that reads like a story out of today's headlines**..."* ~ *Women of Faith Writing Contest*

*"In this meticulously researched novel, **Terry gives readers everything a good novel should have** — a gripping story, an uplifting theme, encouragement in their own faith, and exquisite writing."* ~ *Grace Awards Judges' Panel*

*"The Beloved Daughter is **a beautifully written story**."* ~ *Sarah Palmer, Liberty in North Korea*

Without warning, the officer punched Reuben in the gut. Reuben doubled over as the cop brought his knee up to his face. Reuben staggered.

"You dirty n—." Without warning, the cop whipped out his pistol and smashed its butt against Reuben's head. He crumpled to the ground, where the officer's boots were ready to meet him with several well-placed kicks.

Throwing all rational thoughts aside, Kennedy jumped on his back. Anything to get him to stop beating Reuben. The officer swore and swatted at her. Kennedy heard herself screaming but had no idea what she was saying. She couldn't see anything else, nor could she understand how it was that when her normal vision returned, she was lying on her back, but the officer and Reuben were nowhere to be seen.

Praise for *Policed*
by Alana Terry

"*Policed* could be taken **from the headlines of today's news**." ~ Meagan Myhren-Bennett, *Blooming with Books*

"**A provocative story** with authentic characters." ~ Sheila McIntyre, *Book Reviewer*

"It is important for Christian novelists to address today's issues like police misconduct and racism. Too often writers tiptoe around **serious issues faced by society**." ~ Wesley Harris, *Law Enforcement Veteran*

"Focuses on a prevalent issue in today's society. Alana **pushes the boundaries more than any other Christian writer**." ~ Angie Stormer, *Readaholic Zone*

Simon exhaled as he stretched his arms. "I wish we didn't have to say good-bye." His voice was distant.

Hannah stared at the moon. She would never sit here beside him again in this garden. "There are no good-byes in the kingdom of heaven," she whispered, hoping her words carried the conviction her soul lacked.

Praise for *Torn Asunder*
by Alana Terry

"Filled with suffering, yet ultimately has a **resounding message of hope**." ~ Sarah Palmer, Liberty in North Korea

"Alana has a **great heart for the persecuted church** that comes out in her writing." ~ Jeff King, President of International Christian Concern

"Faith and love are tested beyond comprehension in this **beautifully written Christian novel**." ~ Kathryn Chastain Treat, Allergic to Life: My Battle for Survival, Courage, and Hope

"**Not your average love story** - wrapped in suspense, this story of faith will stop your heart as you hope and weep right along with the characters." ~ Nat Davis, Our Faith Renewed

"Torn Asunder is an **enthralling, heart-aching novel** that calls your heart to action." ~ Katie Edgar, KTs Life of Books

She shook her head. "I don't know. I can't say. I just know that something is wrong here. It's not safe." She clenched his arm with white knuckles. "Please, I can't ... We have to ..." She bit her lip.

He frowned and let out a heavy sigh. "You're absolutely certain?"

She nodded faintly. "I think so."

"It's probably just nerves. It's been a hard week for all of us." There was a hopefulness in his voice but resignation in his eyes.

She sucked in her breath. "This is different. Please." She drew her son closer to her and lowered her voice. "For the children."

"All right." He unbuckled his seatbelt and signaled one of the flight attendants. "I'm so sorry to cause a problem," he told her when she arrived in the aisle, "but you need to get my family off this plane. Immediately."

Praise for *Turbulence*
by Alana Terry

"This book is **hard to put down** and is a **suspenseful roller coaster of twists and turns**." ~ Karen Brooks, *The Book Club Network*

"I've enjoyed all of the Kennedy Stern novels so far, but **this one got to me in a more personal way** than the others have." ~ *Fiction Aficionado*

"I love that the author is **not afraid to deal with tough issues all believers deal with**." ~ Kit Hackett, *YWAM Missionary*

Note: The views of the characters in this novel do not necessarily reflect the views of the author, nor is their behavior necessarily being condoned.

The characters in this book are fictional. Any resemblance to real persons is coincidental. No part of this book may be reproduced in any form (electronic, audio, print, film, etc.) without the author's written consent.

What Dreams May Come
Copyright © 2017 Alana Terry
9781941735466
October, 2017

Cover design by Cover Mint Designs.

Scriptures quoted from THE HOLY BIBLE, NEW INTERNATIONAL VERSION®, NIV® Copyright © 1973, 1978, 1984, 2011 by Biblica, Inc.® Used by permission. All rights reserved worldwide.

www.alanaterry.com

What Dreams May Come

a novel by Alana Terry

CHAPTER 1

Snow fell from the sky at a listless, melancholy pace. Susannah was early, like normal.

Susannah was always early.

Early to graduate high school so that now she was the only teenager she knew who was already this bone-crushingly, soul-wearyingly tired. As if she'd lived four or five decades already.

Dear God, when did I grow so old?

She slipped into her regular spot in the sanctuary. Folks at Orchard Grove Bible Church worked themselves up about a fair number of important issues, pew placement being fairly high up on the list.

Some things would never change. Her aching spirit knew that much with an unyielding certainty. Like the snow. It would keep on falling, keep on covering the drab, muddy winter scene in a beautiful, pristine white, but by tomorrow the landscape would be painted only with grays and browns. Murky, dirt-stained, a smudge of mud and slush, just like it

2

had been when she woke up this morning.

Father, forgive me for grumbling, and help me to be thankful for everything. Even the snow and the mud.

"Good morning, Susannah."

She forced herself to smile at the pinch-nosed woman leaning over the pew in front of her.

"Good morning." Susannah accepted Mrs. Porter's stiff, awkward hug. Most folks at Orchard Grove were content with a handshake from a comfortable three feet away, but since last fall, Susannah had been hugged, embraced, or otherwise enfolded against every bosom of every retired farmer's wife in town.

Mrs. Porter clasped Susannah's hand in hers. "And how are you doing?" She put special emphasis on each word, as if to convey a hidden meaning behind the otherwise mundane question.

Last fall, Susannah might have lied that she was fine, but she knew better now. Knew that Mrs. Porter and those like her expected a certain degree of dignified stoicism. It was a role. The role of the tragically bereaved heroine.

"Thanks so much for asking. I'm feeling ok."

She also attached some unstated significance into this last word, and Mrs. Porter smiled, apparently satisfied at the depth of expression in Susannah's inflection and features.

She held onto her hand for just a second more before adding, "You know, we're all praying for you," and dismissed herself without another word.

Susannah had only recently learned how these promises to pray could abruptly end any conversation. She'd heard it all too often. People had no clue what to say, so after an awkward moment of trying to cheer her up, they simply told her they would remember her in their prayers. Words that might make a newcomer to Orchard Grove grateful, but Susannah had been born and raised in this congregation. She knew enough to suspect that Mrs. Porter and her friends from the church's women's missionary league spent ten minutes gossiping about Susannah's personal life for every two seconds they actually prayed about it.

Did you see the Peters girl in church yesterday? I thought she looked a little pale. Or maybe it was just the dim light.

No, I ran into her at the store just a few days ago, and she was in such a rush to get by, she didn't even notice me.

It's to be expected. You know, she's not even twenty yet, poor thing.

Poor thing ...

Poor thing ...

Susannah glanced at the Bible in her lap, drawing a small dose of comfort as she ran her fingers across the leather cover. *Thank you, Father, for the precious gift of your Word.* The book binding was fancier than she might have liked. She didn't want people to think she was the kind of Christian who paid more attention to her Bible's exterior than the holy words it contained. She also had to fight off a twinge of guilt when she thought about believers in other countries where Scripture was so scarce. Where she could send ten or twelve or twenty paperbacks for the price of this one engraved edition.

But it was a gift from her mother, a gift she would cherish. One of Susannah's only belongings that she planned to take with her when she made it to the mission field.

If she made it to the mission field.

When, God? Is it ever going to happen? Why would you put this desire into my heart if you're never going to bring it to pass?

So many questions. So much silence.

That was all she'd encountered during the past four months. Four trying, exhausting, torturous months.

The din from the foyer increased. Almost everybody at Orchard Grove Bible Church arrived exactly five minutes early. Any sooner and it looked like you were trying too hard. Any later, you'd get glared at as you made your way to find an empty space in the pews. Not that Orchard Grove was overly crowded. There were as many empty seats as filled ones, but they were interspersed so inconveniently across the sanctuary that you would have to step over five or seven or ten different pairs of legs before you could sit.

Orchard Grove's self-imposed punishment for those guilty of tardiness.

Susannah inhaled deeply. *Well, Lord, I'm here. It's been such a long week, but you know how much I'm craving to connect with you today. Please show up, Lord.*

That had been her prayer so often lately. Just asking God to show up.

Crying softly in her room, unable to accept the reality of what had happened. *Please show up, Lord.*

Stroking Kitty's forehead, wishing for some kind of breakthrough. *Please show up, Lord.*

Staring at her phone, knowing she would never hear his voice again, still holding onto some sort of senseless hope that he might call.

Please show up, Lord.

Pastor Greg made his way up front. He and his wife were new to Orchard Grove, but he had already learned that the retired orchardists' and farmers' wives here appreciated —

no, demanded — punctuality. Each week he opened the service at 10:29 and ended at 11:44 without fail. This morning, with about thirty seconds to spare, he smiled at the congregation, and Susannah ran her fingers over her name embossed on her Bible.

Susannah Wesley Peters. A play on words. An homage to some great-uncle or other distant ancestor named Wesley as well as a tribute to Susannah Wesley, the mother of John and Charles. The original Susannah Wesley had never traveled to foreign countries spreading the gospel, never preached to crowds of thousands, never penned hymns or sermons that survived to this day. But she interceded for her sons, who rose up to serve foundational roles in the enlightenment movement on both sides of the Atlantic Ocean. Susannah had lost track of how many times her mother had told her about Mrs. Wesley's commitment to God, how she would flip the skirt of her apron over her head in order to create a mobile prayer closet. How she devoted several hours a day to interceding for her family and maintained regular times of fasting to ask God to use her children to advance his kingdom.

Susannah was grateful for the prayerful example of her namesake, but on days like this, she wondered if praying was the only work for God she'd ever accomplish.

7

WHAT DREAMS MAY COME

Father, don't you see I want to do so much more?

Sometimes the hunger to move from Orchard Grove, to be God's agent of revival and salvation to distant shores was so great it was like a tidal wave ready to surge through her spirit. And when it came crashing down, she couldn't be held responsible for whatever damage was caused by the tsunami of her passion.

And other times, she felt like Orchard Grove's dried-up riverbed, its smooth and rounded rocks the only indication of the rushing waters that had once flowed so powerfully through her.

CHAPTER 2

"Good morning, brother."

Scott glanced at the large clock hanging up in the foyer. "It's afternoon now, isn't it?"

Carl chuckled. "I suppose you're right. I'm still not used to this late service. Well then, good afternoon. How's that?"

Scott shook his pastor's hand. "That's better. And how are you?"

Carl patted his pot belly. "Wife's still got me on that high-fiber, low carb diet of hers. So I'd say that I've been better, because what I'm really craving is a nice steak and baked potato dinner."

Scott smiled. "It's a good thing Christmas is coming up then, isn't it?"

Carl nodded. "You're joining us Christmas Eve, aren't you?"

"Wouldn't miss it. Unless your wife's going to replace her traditional ham with tofu."

Carl chortled. "Not even my Sandy would be that crazy."

He clapped Scott on the back. "You enjoy the service," he said, "and then why don't you come over and eat with us? Call it early supper or late lunch. You can take your pick."

"You sure?" Scott asked. "Wouldn't want to impose last minute."

Carl shook his head. "Not an imposition at all." He grinned and nudged Scott playfully. "Besides, you come over and Sandy's just that much more likely to fix up something sweet for dessert. Not her usual whole wheat almond milk pudding or whatever that health-nut stuff is she's been trying to force feed me."

Scott nodded. "It's a deal." He glanced into the sanctuary, already crowded ten minutes before the start of service. "I guess I better find a seat. You know, you keep preaching the Word like you've been doing, this place is going to need a whole new addition to hold everyone even with the added service."

Carl nodded. "That would be a nice problem to have, wouldn't it, brother?"

Scott glanced around the sanctuary even though he wasn't sure what or who he might be looking for. He'd attended St. Margaret's since arriving back in the States, but he knew less than a dozen members here by name. He still wasn't sure where he fit into the fellowship. A thirty-one-year-old bachelor was something of a congregational misfit. He was too old for the college and careers group, or at least he felt like it the time or two he'd tagged along for Frisbee golf or bowling. He'd spent the first decade of his adult life on the mission field and never settled down long enough to marry, so he didn't belong in any of the Bible studies or prayer groups for couples, parents, or divorcees, either.

He liked St. Margaret's Church. Liked that there were groups for everyone. Everyone, that is, except for singles in that in-between age group where you're not fresh out of the nest but certainly not middle-aged either, where you've spent your entire adult life on the mission field and didn't want to admit how difficult it's been adjusting to a comfortable, relatively stress-free life in the States.

Well, maybe *stress-free* wasn't the right way to put it. For the past two years, Scott had overseen the home office for Kingdom Builders, the mission agency he'd worked with ever since he finished his Bible college certificate. And now that their community engagement manager had left to work at some girls' home up in Vermont, Scott was in charge of the recruitment arm of the ministry as well. Sometimes he jokingly grumbled about working sixty or seventy hours a week on his pitiful missionary salary, but then he realized that even if he had more free time, he wouldn't know what to do with it.

Things were different earlier this year. He'd leave work at 5:30 each day, half an hour before Susannah ended her shift at the assisted living home. Just enough time for him to get home and heat up a quick freezer meal before calling her. Ask about her day. Listen to the smallest details — the Bible verse she'd read that morning or the resident she'd been able to pray with during her shift. The way she chattered about her work, you'd think she'd received a special Mother Theresa-like call from God to change bedsheets and spoon feed the elderly way out there in central Washington.

Until you got her talking about missions. About how she physically hurt sometimes with the burning desire to carry the gospel to the nations. Nobody within a fifty-mile radius could deny that she was called to foreign soil. Not that Scott had actually been within a fifty-mile radius of Susannah Peters, but over the years he had met enough missionaries and prospective workers to get a feel for the kind of believer who would be most effective in the field. The day he'd interviewed Susannah for the Kingdom Builders summer internship, he'd emailed his field director and told him he'd found the next William Carey. Or maybe the next Hudson Taylor, he couldn't remember. Either way, from that first phone conversation on, Scott knew this was a young woman with an incredibly unique calling and passion.

Which was what had made the past four months so complicated.

But that's life for you. If he'd learned anything from his decade overseas, it was that God has a way of keeping you on your toes. Never get too comfortable. Never settle down.

Even Scott's stint in Massachusetts was temporary. His two-year commitment to the home office was up in March, and then he was off to wherever God might lead him next. The Kingdom Builders had fields all across the world, and every single one of them was in need of mission support. When people asked what he did overseas, Scott's go-to response was that he was the "missionary to missionaries," offering spiritual guidance and soul care to the men and women working on the front lines. It was the perfect job for him, really. Perfect for someone with no family connections, nothing tying him down.

Of course, now that he was managing the home office, he was more stationary, but he managed to find reasons to leave the country every three or four months, even if only for short stints.

He enjoyed the lifestyle. Appreciated the freedom. He rented a small bachelor pad in Medford, just a ten-minute walk from the Kingdom Builders home office. With the Boston public transportation system running so efficiently, he never even bothered buying himself a car. The fewer roots he established here in the States, the easier it would be to leave the next time God called him overseas for a long-term placement. It's the way he'd lived for the past decade, the way he'd probably keep on living for the rest of his life. The fact that he could walk into a church service with three thousand other people and realize that there wasn't a single one here who would miss him if he hopped on a plane tomorrow was a small price to pay for the ministry he was able to lead. The life he was able to enjoy.

A life of excitement. Travel. Freedom.

That's the way he wanted it. That's the way it would be.

Scott found an empty seat toward the back of the sanctuary and sat down, wondering what the church service would be like where Susannah Peters lived in Orchard Grove — a quaint, quiet town that he'd never heard of until this time last year.

A quaint, quiet town he'd never been to and no longer had any reason to visit.

CHAPTER 3

Susannah could lose herself so easily in the old hymns that she actually found herself siding with the octogenarians whenever the incendiary classics-versus-contemporary-music debate surfaced at the Orchard Grove church business meetings.

"There is a fountain filled with blood drawn from Immanuel's veins ..."

She could picture her Savior there, hanging on that cross, the blood on his brow like great beads of sorrow and love mingled together, testifying to his mercy and grace.

"And sinners plunged beneath that flood lose all their guilty stains."

She'd grown up at Orchard Grove. Listened to that old piano every Sunday for nearly two decades. There was another church on the other side of town. More contemporary. More young families. She'd tried it out a few times after graduating. Her mom had encouraged her, probably thinking Susannah's chances of finding a suitable

Christian husband were better in a congregation whose average age wasn't over seventy-five. But Susannah had always come back here.

Not that Orchard Grove was perfect. They'd gone through more than their fair share of preachers over the last two decades, weathered a scandal or two, but the church still stood, its steeple pointing proudly heavenward in spite of its peeling paint and weather-worn siding.

God, I feel so comfortable here that sometimes I worry I'm going to stagnate completely.

That was Susannah's biggest fear. Ever since she was twelve, since the day she went on that youth retreat and heard the speaker talk about the unreached people groups of the world, she'd known she was called to the mission field. While still in junior high, Susannah had begged her mom for a set of missionary biographies and promised to write a paper about each one as part of her homeschool studies.

She'd devoured those stories. *God, you were so real to those people. You called them, and they followed you.*

It sounded simple, really, how these men and women would receive their call, obey their call, and make church history in the course of a hundred and twenty pages or less. Susannah had assumed her own life on the mission field would be that straightforward as well.

What went wrong, Lord? She'd asked that question so many times she'd stopped expecting an answer. As far as she could tell, it was an issue on which heaven would remain eternally silent.

The worst part was wondering if it was somehow her own fault. Did she lack the necessary faith? Had she missed God's direction at some point along the way? Allowed other idols to replace her calling? Or maybe the Lord had given up on her. Changed his mind and decided she wasn't fit to become a missionary after all.

"E'er since by faith I saw the stream thy flowing wounds supply, redeeming love has been my theme, and shall be till I die."

As the singing continued, Susannah sighed, ignoring the tears that streaked down her cheeks. The people at Orchard Grove were used to her emotional scenes by now. It was fitting, wasn't it, to still be crying four months later? Even if she wanted to, she couldn't stop herself, couldn't dull the ache in her heart that grew and swelled with each refrain of the familiar hymn.

"And shall be till I die, and shall be till I die …"

Sometimes she wondered if God used the last year to give her a glimpse of heaven and then took it away just to remind her that this world was never meant to be her home.

That was one way to explain the loss. The sadness.

She glanced around the sanctuary at the Christmas decorations, the pine-needle arrangements on the windowsills, the holly and ivy laid over the pulpit. Had it been a full year already?

She was looking for a summer mission program. Nothing more. A way to test out her calling to become a full-time missionary. A chance to step out of her little Orchard Grove comfort zone, to see if she could handle the distance, the separation from her family.

It was only supposed to be one little phone call. A ten-minute conversation where she could ask a few questions she had about the Kingdom Builders mission internship.

She would have never guessed it would lead to so much emptiness and confusion.

God, what did I do wrong? Please tell me so I can repent and be forgiven.

Even as she prayed, the words from the hymn covered over her doubts and sorrows. She knew that after the music ended, she'd have just as many questions, but for now, she would rest in her love for her Savior, no matter how silent he'd remained.

She shut her eyes and lifted her hands, refusing to think about the people behind her who would probably stare.

Redeeming love has been my theme, and shall be till I die.

18

CHAPTER 4

Scott appreciated the extra afternoon service at St. Margaret's Church. For starters, the parking lot after the other two services was too crowded for a pedestrian who didn't want to get hit. Secondly, now Sundays were the closest thing to a true day off he'd experienced in years. Earlier that morning, after going through a few emails he knew he couldn't put off, he'd popped in his earbuds and gone on a jog, with nothing but his thoughts and his Christian rock music to keep him company.

Sometimes he felt guilty. As if a missionary who ministered to nearly a thousand believers around the world should probably lead a more disciplined prayer life. He'd gone through spurts of praying off a list, but after a few weeks of asking God the exact same things for the exact same people, he found it impossible to keep sludging through the monotony. Besides, somewhere in the back of his head was the idea that the most effective prayers were spontaneous anyway. Whenever he went for his morning run, he set off with the best of intentions of spending that time with the Lord but inevitably wasted his mental energy daydreaming.

Usually about Susannah.

The music was his pitiful attempt to tune out her memory, but that was never as effective as he hoped it would be. No matter how high he turned up the volume, her voice was stuck in his head.

It was there this morning when his feet pounded the pavement, sending shock waves up his shins and radiating through his knees.

It was there now when the worship band at St. Margaret's fired up their electric guitars and keyboard, when the music was so loud it surrounded him 360 degrees.

"Jesus, healer of my soul, comfort in my sadness."

He heard the words, but all he could think about was that voice he'd listened to during those countless phone conversations.

Phone conversations long enough, intense enough that the sound of her voice would be forever trapped in his head. Playing and repeating like one of his grandfather's broken records.

Telling him about that day when she was twelve — just a few years ago, really — when she'd received the call to become a missionary.

She was one of the lucky ones. Scott's own path to the mission field was far more mundane. He was about to graduate Bible college with his two-year certificate and didn't know what to do, so his professor suggested he attend the Urbana World Missions Conference, an event bringing together tens of thousands of missions-minded college students and young adults trying to hear God's call on their lives.

Scott loved the Lord. Had loved him ever since he was a little boy sitting on his grandfather's knee, listening to stories about Jesus feeding the five thousand with only a couple loaves of bread and a few fish. The stories were so real and his grandfather's faith so strong that every time Scott caught a whiff of a certain brand of aftershave, part of his spirit was transported back to that day when he knelt by his grandfather's bed and asked Jesus to forgive his sins and become the Lord of his life.

"Son, God's going to do amazing work through you." His grandfather's voice was scratchy, strained after decades of preaching in churches and at old-fashioned tent-revival meetings. So gruff for a man that soft and lovable. "God's going to do amazing work through you."

Maybe it was a proclamation. Maybe it was just the kind of thing adults say to kids after they ask Jesus into their hearts. Either way, Scott wished sometimes his grandfather could see him now. Childish as it might sound, he wanted to make him proud.

"Calm the raging storms in me. Open my eyes and help me see."

The words were simplistic. Scott had never heard the song before, but he could join in with perfect accuracy. He wanted something deeper, something to engage his mind.

Distract him from those omnipresent thoughts of her.

Sometimes he wondered if Susannah Peters existed at all. Was she a living, breathing person or simply an idea?

A phantom?

Sometimes when the disappointment grew too raw, too painful to endure, he told himself he'd made her up completely.

There is no Susannah Peters. She isn't real.

After all, how well can you really know somebody who lives three thousand miles away? No matter how many hours you may spend every evening talking about missions, about theology, about the work of the Holy Spirit in your day-to-day lives, when you say good-night and hang up that phone, you haven't been talking to flesh and blood at all.

You've been fellowshipping with a figment of your imagination. Because Susannah Peters as you think of her isn't real.

So why is her voice in your head when you pray or read your Bible or schedule meetings at work if she doesn't exist? How can you miss her so much so that it becomes a physical ache? How can you mourn over losing someone you never knew?

How can you fall in love with a woman you've never even met?

CHAPTER 5

Susannah's soul was saturated with God throughout the singing. It wasn't until the sermon started that her mind began to wander.

Her stubborn, unruly mind.

God, I'm trying to take every thought captive. I really am. I know I must be a terrible disappointment to you, but please help me focus instead of complaining about all these hopes that can never come true.

That's what made it so hard, though. The fact that whatever she had with Scott — or at least whatever her little girlish mind had thought she'd had with him — was nothing but a dream, an impossibility.

She'd handed Scott over to God four months ago. Four months ago, as an early autumn overtook the fields of Orchard Grove, as the leaves fluttered on the branches before surrendering to their inevitable fate, she sat on her mother's bed, now empty, and poured out her heart to God. Told him that she was willing to give this man back to him.

She didn't realize it at the time, but even as she voiced that prayer of relinquishment, she'd cherished the secret hope that God would see her sacrifice, that he would recognize her willingness to fully surrender to him, and just like he did with Abraham when he placed Isaac on that altar, God would swoop down and tell her, *Never mind. I see now that you will obey me. You passed my test.*

And she and Scott would live happily ever after.

She should have never gotten her hopes set so high in the first place. Hadn't her mother tried to warn her? It wasn't that her mom was against her relationship with Scott. Cautious, maybe, but what mother wouldn't be? Susannah was only eighteen when they met, only a year out of high school. She'd never dated, never lived on her own.

But even though she urged Susannah to proceed with a heavy dose of prayer and discernment, her mom was happy that her daughter had found someone with such a heart for missions. Her only request was that Susannah wait before entering into any sort of official dating relationship until Scott came out to visit and meet them all, the whole family, face-to-face.

Toward the end, it turned out to be only semantics. Scott wasn't her boyfriend, but she loved him. They weren't engaged, but that didn't stop them from dreaming about their future together.

A future serving God on the mission field.

You know, Lord, it's ironic, she'd prayed. *When you first called me to be a missionary, I kept waiting and waiting for you to tell me where I was supposed to go. I read all those biographies, studied the lives of so many servants of yours, and all of them seemed to know so clearly where you wanted them to minister. I waited for you to tell me, but you never did. And now I know why.*

Who would have thought God would bring a man into her life who traveled around the entire world? A missionary to missionaries. That's how Scott described his job. As their relationship grew deeper, as it began to feel more and more certain that they were meant for one another, it all started to make sense. Why God had never given her a specific region he wanted her to serve. It was because he had plans for her to go into all the world. Literally. She wouldn't be preaching the gospel in every single area she visited. Her role would be more like encouragement and prayer support for the missionaries serving with Kingdom Builders, but she'd be involved first-hand in the lives of hundreds of front-line ministers, and she'd be working alongside someone as godly and mature in his faith as Scott.

It was a nice plan for as long as it lasted. Now, those childish fantasies were no more than a source of perpetual embarrassment.

What was I thinking, God? How did you let me give my heart away to someone I'd never even met? I should have listened to Mom. I'm sorry. Will you forgive me now?

She never knew if she was supposed to keep begging for forgiveness until the guilt disappeared, or if she only had to ask once.

She'd done far more confessing in the last four months than in the past ten years combined.

She'd been foolish. That much was certain. Falling in love with a stranger, making plans for a future together before they'd even met. She was young, but was she really that naïve? How could you think you know someone well enough to make a life-changing commitment when you've never sat across the table together and shared a meal? Never held hands and prayed together? Never worshiped in the same church building or even the same time zone?

Scott was all the way out on the East Coast, and whenever he'd tried to fly out to Washington to visit her, something had come up. Talk about a warning sign. God was telling her even back then that it would never work, but she was too stubborn to listen, too head-over-heels in love to pay him any heed.

I'm sorry, Lord. Please give me your wisdom so I don't make such foolish decisions again.

She stared at the leather-bound Bible in her lap. She'd have no idea what Pastor Greg preached about by the time his sermon ended. Yet another sin she'd have to repent of later.

Some people had the gift of prayer or the gift of evangelism.

It appeared Susannah was gifted in confession. She certainly had made enough mistakes lately to give herself the extra practice.

She opened to the front page of her Bible. Her mom's handwriting was so distinct Susannah could shut her eyes and still visualize the exact height of each curve, the angle of each slant.

To my sweet daughter on her graduation day. "'For I know the plans I have for you,' declares the Lord."

Love, Mom

That was it. No long, flowery letter, no lengthy prayer or written blessing. No poignant words of wisdom. Probably because at the time, Mom assumed she'd have decades to keep on teaching Susannah. Keep on mentoring her. Discipling her. Encouraging her in the faith.

Who would have guessed it would all end like this?

You knew, God. For some people, it's comforting to believe that nothing happens out of your will. Unfortunately, Susannah didn't see it that way. From her vantage point, God had known what was about to happen and had done absolutely nothing to warn her. To prepare her for the trials and heartaches ahead.

Everything had been going so well. Perfectly. Scott had finally found a free weekend when the Kingdom Builders wouldn't need him for any last-minute trips. He'd booked a flight into Spokane. Susannah was giddy with excitement. It had been almost nine months since their first phone call. Who would have thought that what should have been a ten or fifteen-minute interview would have turned into such a deep, abiding friendship?

And more than a friendship, even though her mom told her she wasn't supposed to give away her heart until she'd met him face to face. Maybe Susannah hadn't done a great job at that part, but she'd tried. And as excited as she was, she wasn't the least bit worried about meeting Scott. There was nothing in her spirit warning her that he might not be the man she expected, the man she'd grown to love. Some things you just know, even if you don't have a logical reason to explain why you're so certain.

At least, that's what she thought at the time as her

whole family joyfully prepared to welcome Scott into their home for an extended weekend. Well, not quite into their home since he'd be spending the nights at the parsonage with the pastor and his wife, but it was basically understood that his waking hours would be with Susannah and her family.

She'd never felt so lucky, never thought before how proud she was to be part of such a loving, close-knit home. Even Derek, her stepdad of only a few months, asked dozens of questions about Scott's likes and dislikes as he tried to plan a way for them to spend some man-to-man time together. When he heard Scott was a runner, he decided to invite him on the trail alongside the dried-up riverbed through Orchard Grove, and a few weeks before the visit Derek increased his regular workout routine so he could keep up with a "younger man."

Nobody mentioned that Scott was closer to her stepdad's age than he was to Susannah's.

In the meantime, her mom had gone over meal plan after meal plan until she had every calorie for the weekend tracked down in her overstuffed daily planner. "Now, I know the two of you are going to want some time alone together, but the rules are just the same now as they were when you were in high school. No boys in the bedroom, and even when you want your privacy, it's going to be with either Derek or me at home at all times, understood?"

Susannah was happy to accept her mother's terms. She'd never kissed a boy before, never even held hands with one. And even though she didn't want to be presumptuous enough to expect Scott to kiss her, she was simultaneously afraid he would try to and terrified that he wouldn't. How was it possible that they'd talked about the countries they'd visit as missionaries once they got married but they'd never discussed how physically affectionate they'd be when he came out to meet her and her family?

She glanced once more at her mother's writing. *"For I know the plans I have for you," declares the Lord.* God wasn't surprised by any of the events of the past four months.

Father, I don't mean to complain, and I'm sorry for being so ungrateful lately. But if you knew what was going to happen to my family, if you knew exactly what was coming, if it really was part of your plan for my life all along, couldn't you have offered me some little warning sign?

Was that too much to ask?

She looked at the page again, but the message remained as succinct as before, and heaven as always was silent.

CHAPTER 6

Sometimes Scott wondered if pastors who'd worked as long as Carl got tired of December. Was it hard to preach four or five Christmas sermons a year and find something new to point out each time? Or after several decades behind the pulpit did you just stop trying to be original?

Today's sermon was fairly standard. Scott spent more time studying the advent arrangement than watching Carl. This week's candle stood for joy, which for some reason kept reminding Scott of the way he'd laughed when Susannah told him her middle name. Knowing she came from a fairly conservative Christian home, he had expected something more standard like Joy or Grace. When she told him she'd been named after the historical Susannah Wesley, he'd chuckled into his phone. "So that explains why you're so good at praying."

Even without seeing her face, he knew his comment had flustered her.

"I'm not good or bad. It's just something we're supposed to do."

He wouldn't allow her to demure so easily. "Maybe, but you've got to admit that some people do it better than others." And from that moment on, he realized how well the name suited her. Susannah Wesley Peters. He wondered how it would sound once they got married. Susannah Wesley Phillips. It rolled off the tongue well, and she wouldn't have to change her initials or give up having an apostolic surname.

Of course, that was all in the past. So long ago now that he couldn't remember if they'd had that conversation about her middle name before or after he'd bought his plane ticket to Washington. After months of saving up, scouring the discount flight webpages, and then rescheduling twice, he was finally going to see her.

Meet the woman who'd captured his heart.

It was still hard to believe. He'd prayed years earlier and told God he'd remain single unless the Lord brought someone into his life who shared the same passion for the mission field as he did. He'd spent so many years alone he started to worry he wouldn't know how to join his life with someone else's. Wouldn't a wife nag him about making his bed or keeping the toilet seat down?

Besides, there was something exciting about his lifestyle, knowing that in a week he could be on a plane to South Africa or get called to speak at a conference in western

Russia. Where would he find a woman who felt the same way about that sort of spontaneity? And what about kids? Even if he met a girl willing to travel the whole world over by his side, what would happen if or when children came into the fold? Was he just supposed to retire? The last two years on home-office duty would have bored him completely out of his mind if he hadn't had Susannah to talk to. They did the math once. If you were to assume two hours on the phone a night (a conservative estimate), plus a few extra hours on the weekend, they'd spent somewhere over four hundred hours on the phone together just in the first six months. More than the equivalent of two and half straight weeks doing nothing but talking. He finally bought an external battery for his phone so he could stay connected without having to plug his cell in halfway through the conversation.

Nights certainly had been quiet lately in comparison.

Quiet nights and a cell that could hold its charge for three or four days at a time.

His heart still raced when the phone rang. Even though he knew it wouldn't be her. Even though it hadn't been her for four months. Email was worse. Refreshing his inbox twenty times an hour. Facing the bitter sense of disappointment each time he remembered he'd never hear from her again.

Sometimes he had nightmares. Nightmares where she wanted to talk to him but his phone wouldn't connect. He'd try to pick up, but it wouldn't go through. The worst part wasn't missing the call itself but fearing that she'd take his silence as rejection.

Fearing that she'd move on.

Find someone else.

She was so young. So passionately in love with the Lord.

It was fruitless to imagine what might have happened between them under different circumstances. But still, he hoped she wouldn't replace him right away. It was selfish of him, really. He should wish her all the happiness in the world. Women like Susannah were made for family life. For marriage and motherhood. While it was possible for him to imagine himself remaining perpetually single, he knew Susannah would one day find a husband.

A husband who would take care of her.

Who wouldn't drag her away from the family that needed her.

A husband who wasn't him.

He'd known. He didn't admit it to himself at the time, but he'd known she'd end up breaking up with him. If you can call it a breakup when you haven't even met face to face.

35

Susannah's heart was for the nations. He'd picked up on that during the first phone interview when all he was supposed to do was answer a few of her questions about the Kingdom Builders summer internship program. Which is why he thought they might be a perfect fit, but after everything that happened last fall, he couldn't have asked her to leave. Shouldn't have expected her to do anything but stay out there in Orchard Grove, serving God in her little quiet sphere.

He should have been the one to end things. It would have been easier on her. After those hundreds of hours on the phone, those thousands of pages worth of emails, he knew her so well. Well enough to know that she would feel guilty now. He wanted to tell her that he understood, that he'd freely forgive her if there was anything to forgive.

She was stronger than he was. She realized her duty was to her God and her family, and she was devoted enough to deny herself the one thing that could make her truly happy. Scott had seen it coming, but he didn't have the emotional fortitude to finalize things like she did. Her resolve and her submission to the Holy Spirit put him to shame.

I'm sorry.

He composed a dozen emails in his head a week, some begging her to change her mind, some praising her for her heart of surrender, most just telling her how much he missed her.

36

Pastor Carl was continuing on in his Christmas sermon on the theme of joy. *"Weeping may stay for the night, but rejoicing comes in the morning."* God must be using figurative language because Scott had woken up to over a hundred lonely mornings since the last time he talked with Susannah, and rejoicing still seemed so far out of reach.

Did she think about him? Was she sitting in that little country church way out in Orchard Grove, Washington, right now, wondering how he was?

Or maybe she already found someone else. Jewels like Susannah wouldn't stay unattached forever. Was her stepdad still in the picture? Would he offer his assistance, help steer her away from predators? She was so trusting. So trusting and still so young. She'd given her heart to Scott so readily, a testimony to her innocent nature. She'd loved him months before he felt the freedom in his spirit to talk to her about courtship. She hadn't said so, but he had learned how to read her so well that by the time he finally found the courage to tell her he loved her, the question wasn't whether she loved him back but what to do now that their affection was out in the open.

She was created for intimacy. Designed to share her heart with those around her. It's what made her so fulfilled working at that assisted living home. It's what gave her such a passion for the poor and destitute around the globe, lost souls who'd never heard the name of Jesus Christ.

And ultimately, it was that same loving, gentle nature that forced her to break off communication. Tell him things could never work between them.

He still had that ticket he'd printed up for his flight to Spokane. Still looked at it sometimes as if to prove to himself that somewhere in the country there really was a place called Orchard Grove, even if it was too small to show up on any but the most detailed of maps. That somewhere in that itty bitty town was a young woman who'd loved him enough to invite him into her heart, into her life.

That Susannah Wesley Peters was a living, breathing woman he'd loved in return but now would never get the chance to meet.

CHAPTER 7

Susannah watched the snow falling outside the window, disappointed that she wasn't paying more attention to the preaching. Greg, unlike any other pastor who made his way through the doors of Orchard Grove Bible Church, didn't believe that every sermon in advent season had to be about the birth of Jesus. Susannah wasn't sure how the traditionalists would feel about a December series through the life of King David, but she had her suspicions.

Father God, protect and watch over Pastor Greg. Bless his ministry, and allow him to continue to lead this church with wisdom and discernment.

She'd learned years ago to intercede for her pastors regularly. Orchard Grove Bible Church couldn't be the easiest of congregations to serve, especially for a young newlywed like him.

The soft flurry outside was turning into a full-fledged storm. The snow covered everything. The mud, the litter, even the tire tracks in the parking lot. Some folks complained about Orchard Grove's lack of aesthetics, but Susannah had never lived anywhere else, rarely traveled, and lacked any reference point for comparison. She wondered what Massachusetts looked like. Strange to think that she and Scott had spent almost a year talking, and she didn't even know about New England weather.

There she was distracted again. *I'm so sorry, God. One day, I'm going to get him out of my mind. But I need your help.*

It was times like these that she missed her mom the most poignantly. Christmas was less than two weeks away, but what kind of celebration would they have? She hadn't shopped for any presents. She didn't have time, let alone the money. She'd been unemployed for the past four months, not that she had any time to miss her job at Winter Grove Assisted Living. Life was busier now than it'd ever been. She couldn't remember how many days had passed since she'd taken her last shower.

Now that she was gone, Susannah developed an even greater appreciation for her mother and all the sacrifices she'd made for her family.

Sacrifices. There was a word Susannah wouldn't miss if it disappeared from every dictionary in the English-speaking world.

ALANA TERRY

Sacrifices. Because keeping your promises was more important than chasing fantasies.

Because serving contentedly where God's called you was infinitely more satisfying than yearning to be somewhere else. Or so she was told.

Lord, I know you ask us to lay down our lives for others, but I feel like there's nothing left for me to give. I'm so empty.

As parched as the Orchard Grove riverbed. She could still remember being a little girl, tossing pebbles into the rushing water. How many years had passed since the river dried up? Ten? Twelve?

And would it ever run again?

Pastor Greg was near the end of his sermon. She could tell because of the way the orchardists in the front rows began clearing their throats and checking their watches. The way the few children in the pews grew more and more fidgety. The way her own heavy heart reminded her it was time to go home.

That's what she hated about herself the most, what she hoped God would change more than anything else.

Lord, I used to love being with my family. What's happened to me?

She wished she knew. Had she taken her entire annual quota of love and poured it out on a stranger, a stranger who

41

turned out to be nothing but a stumbling block?

Before she met Scott, she had never begrudged her family anything. Never complained. It was her mother who worried. Her mother who signed Susannah up for music lessons and dance classes and homeschool co-ops, all in the name of giving her as much of a normal childhood as possible. It took years for her mom to realize that Susannah more than anything wanted to be at home. It was part of her nature to love. Part of her ingrained, God-given personality to nurture those around her, to tend to those who needed her.

That's why she was such a good fit for the Winter Grove Assisted Living Home. Changing bedpans, cleaning messes, helping the weak while still protecting their dignity. When in her life had Susannah not known instinctively that her job was to care for others?

Some people called it a gift of compassion. For Susannah, it came as simply and as easily as breathing.

Or at least it had.

That's the irony, God. This is the future I'd always pictured for myself. It's just that I didn't expect it to come so soon.

Not before she'd had the chance to live her own life.

Not before she'd served God for twenty or thirty years on foreign soil.

Not before she'd fallen in love, gotten married, nurtured and cared for children of her own.

Susannah was living the life she'd always dreamed of.

The problem was she was living it three or four decades earlier than she'd originally planned.

CHAPTER 8

Scott knew from experience that Pastor Carl and his family wouldn't be ready to leave St. Margaret's for at least forty-five minutes after the service ended. This was one of those times when having a vehicle of his own might be convenient. If Susannah were here instead of him, she could probably sit down in one of the pews with her Bible and pass two or three hours before even thinking of glancing up at the clock.

Scott wasn't like that, which was one reason why he'd been both drawn toward her and intimidated as well. Sometimes he wondered if things would have turned out differently if Susannah were older. How could he have expected to uproot someone that young from the family she loved? Many women would have never stuck around, would have left Orchard Grove the moment the opportunity presented itself.

But not Susannah. After just their first week of emailing, even before that decisive phone interview, Scott could tell what a nurturing, compassionate person she was. And it was no surprise, given her family situation. Growing up the way she did, she would have either become the Florence Nightingale of Orchard Grove or she would have fled town the moment she graduated high school.

He should have known even then. The thought of Susannah leaving her family, a family that needed her more than any of them realized, went against the very core of her personality. Sure, he had heard her talk about the mission field, had himself been inspired by her passion. But not even the intensity of her call overseas or whatever romance had started to flourish between them could tear her away.

Scott couldn't blame her for that. As easy as it would be, as much as it might help him move past his sorrow and disappointment, he couldn't blame Susannah for staying home any more than he could blame a landed fish for returning to the sea.

He sighed. The church was emptying out. He had his phone in his pocket, but he wouldn't check his email. Susannah wouldn't write him. Not today. Not ever.

Ironic, really. He had fallen in love with her gentle spirit, her giving heart. And it was her sacrificial selflessness, the very essence of Susannah Peters' character he admired so deeply, that had ultimately pulled them apart.

45

"I made a promise to my mom," she had explained that day last August. He didn't have to see her face. He knew just from the quiver in her voice that she was struggling to hold back tears. Tears that wouldn't fall until she told him what she had decided and then said good-bye.

He wondered if she still cried. Did she dream about him like he dreamed about her?

Did she sense the injustice of her situation? Did she grow resentful of the family that had stripped and starved her of all hope of happiness?

No. She was too gentle. Too full of love. Any sadness she felt after cutting Scott out of her life would only sweeten her disposition, offering a depth and intensity to the young woman he'd fallen in love with.

He ignored the gnawing emptiness in his chest and made his way into the church library. His stomach rumbled. His knees ached after his morning run, but the physical discomforts were a welcome distraction from the heaviness and pain that had seeped into his soul.

CHAPTER 9

Finally. The last *amen.* Susannah was ashamed of her relief when the service ended. Not that she was eager to return home. She just had such a hard time sitting still. She could hardly recognize herself these days. Good thing her mom couldn't see her. At least, Susannah hoped not.

"Real quickly before we dismiss," Pastor Greg said, interrupting her unruly thoughts, "Grandma Lucy has asked for the opportunity to close us in prayer today."

Susannah knew what that meant. She resisted the urge to twist around in her seat to check the time on the clock. Had Grandma Lucy spoken in church since Greg and his wife came to town? She didn't think so, which probably explained why the pastor looked so innocent and unsuspecting.

Grandma Lucy took the mic. Even though none of her grandchildren attended services at Orchard Grove anymore, Susannah couldn't remember her being called anything besides Grandma Lucy, just like she couldn't remember a time when she didn't have shock white hair or wear the same style of nylon blouse with oversized collars.

Susannah let out a deep breath.

God, I know you love that woman so much, and you've given her a spiritual fire and intensity that really is refreshing to see in a church like this. But can you please tell her to keep it a little shorter than normal today? I can't be late.

Derek was expecting her. She shut her eyes just for a moment.

"Thank you, Pastor Greg." Grandma Lucy's voice hadn't changed since Susannah was a little girl — still full of cracks and warbles on account of her age and conviction that only hinted at her spiritual intensity.

Grandma Lucy glanced around the sanctuary. Without knowing why, Susannah looked down at her lap.

"I'd like to end the service with a word of prayer today," Grandma Lucy began. "God is so good, isn't he? During the sermon, he just kept reminding me over and over of his great and powerful love that he has not only for me but for every single one of us here, not to mention every single lost and hurting soul in the entire world. It was all I could do to keep from jumping to my feet and shouting *hallelujah*."

Susannah tried to calm her restless spirit.

ALANA TERRY

*Lord, you speak to Grandma Lucy so often that it's like
she's having one long continuous conversation with you
each and every day. But here I am begging for a single word
from you, a single hint of your presence. It's been so long
since I've felt you near me. Is it too much to ask you for one
small glimpse of your love, one small taste of your glory?
It's been so long, Lord.*

Pastor Greg, perhaps realizing that he had relinquished
all control over the service along with that microphone,
edged a little closer to Grandma Lucy, but she didn't seem
to notice.

"I want to close us today with a blessing from the book
of Isaiah. *Comfort, comfort my people, says your God,*"
Grandma Lucy quoted. "*Speak tenderly to Jerusalem, and
proclaim to her that her hard service has been completed,
that her sin has been paid for, that she has received from the
Lord's hand double for all her sins.*"

It was Grandma Lucy's way, the same pattern as always,
reciting verses from Scripture and then ad-libbing until
prayer and preaching and exhortation were all wrapped up in
one package.

Susannah glanced over at the restless faces around her,
the shuffling feet, the children who acted as if they might
spontaneously combust if they had to sit still a moment

49

longer. What was it about Grandma Lucy that made people so nervous? Was it because everyone but the unsuspecting pastor knew that ten or twenty minutes could pass from the time she started speaking until she said her last *amen*? No, there had to be more to it than just restless minds and hungry stomachs. Maybe some were afraid that through some special revelation of the Holy Spirit, the old woman might divine their hidden sins and struggles.

For Susannah, it went deeper than the fear of exposure. Grandma Lucy had spent her life serving God, had grown up as a missionary kid in China, had spent several years serving in the Middle East as an adult, and had returned on multiple missions to Asia smuggling Bibles far into her old age. But here she was in Orchard Grove — in a town where just about everybody had access to the gospel if they wanted to hear it, in a church that held her emboldened prayer times suspect at best — and she was spiritually thriving.

What's her secret, God? How can she stand living here? And when will I ever learn to be content like her?

CHAPTER 10

"I thought I might find you in here." Carl's booming voice pierced through the silence of the church library.

Scott looked up from the book he'd been reading.

"What you got there?" Carl asked.

He held it up. "*Revolution in World Missions.* You read it?"

Carl smiled. "Only about five times. You set? Sandy and Woong are waiting in the car."

Scott followed his pastor out the door. Carl fumbled in his pockets and muttered, "Now where did I put those keys?"

Once they reached his Honda, Carl eased himself into the driver's seat, and Scott hopped in the back. Carl's wife Sandy turned around to smile at him. "I'm so glad you decided to join us for lunch."

"I can't find my keys," Carl grumbled, and Sandy pointed to the ignition, where they dangled from a New Orleans Saints keychain.

"Hey, Mr. Scott," Woong piped up. "Do you wanna hear a joke?"

Scott smiled. He'd never felt all that comfortable around kids, but for some reason, Carl and Sandy's son was one of the exceptions. "Sure. Tell me a good joke."

"Ok." Woong scrunched up his face in thought before finally reciting, "Knock, knock."

"Who's there?"

"Isaiah."

"Isaiah who?"

"Isaiah prayer for you every day. Get it?"

Scott let out the expected chuckle. "That's a good one."

"Now it's your turn," Woong stated as Carl pulled out of the parking lot.

"My turn to tell you a joke?"

Woong nodded. Scott thought back to his two years at Bible school. He'd learned some riddles there. If only he could remember one.

"Ok, how about this." He smiled at Woong's eager expression. "What were Goliath's last words?"

"Goliath?" Woong repeated.

"Yeah. Goliath. You know, the giant David killed with the slingshot and the stone."

"What were his last words?" Woong squinted and scratched his cheek. Scott had never met a kid with more expressive features. "I don't know. I give up."

Scott beamed. "Ok. Goliath's last words were, 'Such a thing never entered my head before.'" He laughed before he realized the rest of the car was silent.

"I don't get it." Woong frowned, but he didn't wait for Scott to explain the punchline. "But now it's my turn. Dad told this one in church last Sunday, so if you heard it then just pretend like you didn't, all right? How did Moses make his coffee? He-*brews* it."

It was a short drive to Carl and Sandy's home in Medford, especially in the middle of a Sunday afternoon. By the time Carl pulled his Honda into the garage, Scott realized two things. First, the Lindgrens were even bigger saints than he'd realized for the patience they showed Woong, who apparently was only quiet when he was eating or sleeping.

Second, if Scott tried really hard and had enough distracting him, he could go a full twelve minutes without letting thoughts of Susannah Peters creep into his mind and darken his mood.

CHAPTER 11

"The Lord takes such great delight in you," Grandma Lucy spoke into the microphone. Susannah tried to gauge how Pastor Greg felt about his renegade congregant, but his expression was a blend of polite stoicism and patience — perfectly indecipherable.

"He rejoices over you with his singing. His delight is in you, the workmanship of his hands, the masterpiece of the artist of artists, the great author and finisher of our faith when we put our trust in him."

The words were a blend of Scripture verses and Grandma-Lucy-style embellishments. Most of the time, Susannah found these sorts of impromptu service closings encouraging. She liked to think that one day she might have Grandma Lucy's boldness and conviction. But today, she was only tired. Tired and ready to get home.

To the family that was waiting for her.

"Blessed are those who mourn," Grandma Lucy quoted, "for they will be comforted. Blessed are those who weep tears of sorrow and grief."

Susannah knew those kinds of tears all too well, had experienced them in the most inopportune times since August. That day had started perfectly. It's strange how she remembered the gorgeous weather so vividly, that unexpected cool spell bringing an early end to the merciless heat of summer. Scott's flight was due in five days, but by the bustle at home, you'd think he was half an hour late.

Susannah's mom decided to make Amish friendship bread for his arrival. She'd prepped the starter ten days early like always, but she'd underestimated the Washington summer heat. Susannah came home from her shift at Winter Grove to find her mom scrubbing yeasty flour off the kitchen cupboards after her Ziploc bag had burst, exploding starter in every direction.

"God must be punishing me for my vanity," her mom lamented. "It's what I deserve for trying to show off my baking skills to your friend."

It always struck Susannah as strange to hear Scott described as *her friend*, as if he was nothing but another student from youth group or homeschool co-op who was stopping by for a quick visit instead of the man she hoped to marry who was traveling all the way across the country just to meet her.

Susannah helped her mom clean the mess and offered to buy a bag of starter from Safe Anchorage Farms. "Connie always has some batches ready to sell."

"I know that," her mom sighed, "but I really wanted to do it from scratch."

Susannah did her best to cheer her mother up. "It will be more authentic this way. Didn't Connie actually get her original starter from the Amish to begin with?"

Her mom shrugged and pecked her on the cheek. "You always have such a positive attitude. But you're tired. You just got home from work and haven't even changed your clothes. You go rest up, and I'll stop by Safe Anchorage. This is my mistake, and I'm willing to clean up after myself."

Susannah should never have let her go. Should have argued that they didn't need any friendship bread. That Scott would have been happy with week-old dry bread rolls.

And if her mom still insisted, Susannah should have gotten the starter herself. She needed to pick up some more stationary anyway, and Safe Anchorage always had such nice journals in their gift shop.

She should never have allowed her mother out that door.

But instead, she handed her mom the keys. Gave her a quick kiss on the cheek. "Oh," Susannah added as her mom grabbed her purse, "did Kitty get her afternoon snack?"

"No, hon. I'm sorry. I heard the bag explode and was so busy cleaning it up that I lost track of time. I know you had a long day, but would you mind taking care of it while I'm gone?"

"Of course not." Another hug. How could she have taken that loving physical contact for granted for all those years? "Drive safely."

That's the part Susannah couldn't remember if she'd said or not. Maybe it was just her memory getting that goodbye mixed up with the hundreds, the thousands of others over the years. Maybe it was her subconscious way of trying to assuage her guilt.

She hadn't kept her mom from getting in that car, but she'd told her to be careful ...

And then Mom was gone. As simple as that. Simple as driving a few miles out to Baxter Loop to buy some starter for the Amish friendship bread she wanted to make to impress her daughter's cross-country *friend*.

Grandma Lucy continued on in her prayer, but Susannah's mind was stuck on that one single verse she'd quoted earlier.

"Blessed are those who mourn, for they shall be comforted."

Susannah didn't want to sound cynical, didn't want to sound like she doubted the Bible, but she was starting to wonder how long that comfort was supposed to linger before it finally arrived.

CHAPTER 12

"So tell me, Scott, have you gotten back in touch with your friend in Washington?" Sandy pulled Tupperware out of the fridge while Woong set the table.

Scott sat across from his pastor and stared at the Lazy Susan in front of him. "No, haven't heard anything." He didn't like the way his voice sounded so flat, didn't like the sense of finality he heard in his own words.

Sandy clucked her tongue. "Well, maybe it's all for the best. God's got his plans. We know that much."

Scott nodded absently. Carl and Sandy had followed his unorthodox romance from the beginning, starting with that first phone call. Of course, he and Susannah hadn't talked about any sort of relationship at the time, but Scott spent the entire next week trying and failing to get her out of his mind. He couldn't talk to anyone at the Kingdom Builders home office. There weren't specific rules against falling in love with potential recruits, but he doubted he'd be encouraged to pursue anything with Susannah on account of her age if nothing else.

He'd met lots of girls over the years. Bible college was full of them, and he'd had a few casual relationships that never seemed to go anywhere. Some potential dates ended up intimidated by his single-minded focus for world missions. It sounded romantic, traveling forty-eight weeks out of every year and ministering to missionaries across the globe, but when it came right down to it, most girls he met were interested in a more traditional way of life. Steady job, two kids, nice house in the suburbs, a dog or two thrown in for good measure.

During his first few years on the field, Scott felt uneasy, unsettled. Asking God when his time would come to meet the woman he could spend the rest of his life with. Finally, he grew to accept and even appreciate the single lifestyle. He meditated often on Paul's words, how an unmarried Christian can remain focused and devoted to the Lord instead of always worrying about pleasing their spouse.

He could have remained contentedly single for the rest of his life.

Until he met Susannah.

She wasn't on social media. Her family was conservative by just about every definition of the word, and she was still so young. He hadn't even known what she looked like when he stumbled through that first awkward confession.

Two months after their initial phone interview, two months of daily emails and nearly daily conversations by phone, and Scott finally had to tell her the truth. Tell her that he was falling in love with her. That he wanted to meet her.

She hadn't said that she loved him back, and he didn't ask her to. Her mom was strict. Cautious about her daughter's long-distance relationship with someone she'd never met. Scott wasn't supposed to know, but her mom had called one of his supervisors at work to make sure that Susannah hadn't been talking to a serial killer or sex offender or pathological liar.

Even once it become known around the home office that Scott was in some sort of unofficial relationship with one of the summer internship recruits, it had been Carl and Sandy he talked to most.

"I've never met another woman like her," Scott had said, and Carl never once brought up the fact that technically he still hadn't met her.

At some point after his confession, he and Susannah started exchanging snail mail in addition to the daily emails and phone calls. That's when he finally received his first picture of her.

He'd carried it to Carl and Sandy's house to proudly display. Nobody at the home office told him to give up on his relationship with Susannah, but his well-meaning co-workers didn't understand. Didn't get how two people who'd never seen each other could know each other that deeply.

Could love each other that sincerely.

Susannah had mailed him a copy of her senior photo. She had written a verse from Psalms on the back: *My soul yearns, even faints for the courts of the Lord.* Sandy had gushed. Had fawned over those large, brown eyes, the long, golden hair. Carl patted him on the back and congratulated him. Scott was no longer in love with just a voice.

His angel now had a face.

It was just a month or two later that he called her mom to ask if he could fly out to visit. Mrs. Peters was getting ready for her own wedding, said the timing was wrong, asked him to wait patiently, reminded him that she still wanted her daughter to keep from giving away her heart.

As if someone as loving and compassionate as Susannah could withhold her affection.

He'd tried again over Easter break. Things had settled down. Susannah's mom was married, and they'd all moved in with her new husband. Now that she didn't have the stress of planning a wedding on her shoulders, Susannah's mom was warm and hospitable when she invited him out for a visit.

It would have been perfect if the Kremlin hadn't tightened their anti-proselytizing laws and sent everyone from the Russian field into a dizzying tailspin. Scott was needed in Moscow, then Petersburg.

The Washington trip was postponed again.

And again.

He should have realized it was God's hand all along, but he was too stubborn. Maybe if he had backed off earlier, he wouldn't be hurting so much right now.

Just five days before he was due to fly out last August, Susannah's mom was killed in a car crash. At first, he tried to change his ticket so he could leave immediately. Stay by Susannah's side during those first tumultuous, grief-stricken days. But she told him she needed time with her family, so he stuck to the original plan.

And then, just twelve hours before his flight was scheduled to take off, she called him. He could tell from her voice she'd been crying. His arms ached with the longing to wrap her up and shield her from her pain and trauma. He was ready to comfort her. Ready to pour out all his love on her. To walk through this tragedy by her side.

But she told him to wait. Said something about her sister not doing well. Telling him it wasn't a good time for him to come visit after all.

He should have gone. Even now, he wondered what might have changed if he'd followed his gut, the part of him that knew she longed to be with him as much as he yearned to be with her.

But he figured they'd already waited so long. What could a few more days hurt?

And then she'd called the afternoon of her mom's funeral. He was so blinded by his own foolish dreams. Otherwise he might have been prepared.

"I can't see you," she'd said.

At first, he thought maybe her stepdad was the problem. It wasn't like Derek had played any major role in her life. They'd only shared a house for a few months at the time of her mother's death.

But it wasn't Derek.

"I made my mom a promise," she explained.

He should have seen it coming. Instead, her words rattled him as much as a three-hundred-foot drop on a trans-Atlantic flight.

That was the last time he'd spoken with Susannah Wesley Peters, the woman he loved.

The woman whose engagement ring sat in a box on his nightstand.

The woman he'd planned to propose to.

CHAPTER 13

"The good Lord will raise you up on eagles' wings. He will cover you with his feathers and offer you his comfort once more."

Comfort. What kind of comfort could Susannah expect after all she'd been through?

Grandma Lucy was still going strong, without offering any hint that she was getting tired or preparing to wind down her speech. "The Lord is faithful, and *he who began a good work in you will carry it on to completion.*"

It was a verse Susannah had been thinking about a lot lately. *Carry it on to completion.* Well, maybe for some people. Strong believers like Grandma Lucy, who spent most of their lives on the mission field serving God. Or Scott, with his passion for the lost guiding everything he did.

Susannah might have been like that. She wanted to be like that. Wanted to have the same kind of faith that would sustain her as she traveled to the remotest parts of the earth, following God wherever his Spirit might lead. But she'd made a promise. A promise she refused to break.

A promise that would dictate the rest of her life.

God, I'm so sorry for complaining. I hate that I'm becoming so resentful.

A promise. A promise she'd been happy to give when her mom was healthy, when the future was bright, when it seemed like Susannah would have decades ahead of her. Decades of freedom, adventure, love.

Why did you have to take her away so soon? Susannah prayed as the uninvited, ugly thought she'd been fighting crept up into her consciousness: *It shouldn't have been Mom.*

It was a hideous thought. A hideous thing to wish, but there it was, staring her in the face like a gangrene infection.

It shouldn't have been Mom.

She let out a choppy breath as Grandma Lucy recited the familiar passage from Isaiah. "Those who hope in the LORD will renew their strength. They will soar on wings like eagles; they will run and not grow weary, they will walk and not be faint."

Over the course of her life, Susannah's mom had made her memorize dozens, probably hundreds of Bible verses. Learning Scripture was as regular a part of the family routine as praying before meals or practicing math facts every day. Her mom was so strong in the faith. Susannah still remembered how strange she'd felt as a little girl the first time she heard her mom cry.

Susannah was five or six, and they had just pulled into the garage after gymnastics classes. Susannah jumped out and stood watching while Mom helped her sister out of her car seat.

"Mom, how old was I when I started walking?"

Mom, somewhat distracted, answered, "I don't know, hon. Around a year."

Susannah crossed her arms. Watched the familiar sight of Mom unbuckling Kitty. Making sure not to tangle the seatbelt around her.

"Well, how old's Kitty gonna be when she learns to walk?"

Mom stopped and stared at her. Had she asked something wrong?

Unease and a hint of unexplained embarrassment warmed Susannah's tummy, and she tried to think of what she could say to cover over any mistake she might have made. "I mean, I was just wondering. Because I was thinking she always smiles so big at gymnastics that I think she'll like it once she gets old enough to do it herself."

Mom sighed. "That's why we take her to her physical therapy. You know that, babe."

Susannah frowned. "Yeah, but ..."

Mom shushed her with a quick, "We'll talk about this inside," and Susannah clammed up instinctively. Automatically, still unable to erase the strange shame in her belly.

Later that afternoon, while Kitty was napping and Susannah was helping mix some chocolate chip cookie batter, Mom said, "Now about your question earlier."

Susannah's cheeks heated. She could tell her curiosity had somehow hurt Mom's feelings. She stared into the bowl.

Stir, mix, stir.

"There's something you need to know about Kitty." Mom was using the same reverent tone she used when she talked about God or Jesus or the Bible or Daddy up in heaven.

Stir, mix, mix.

"Kitty's a really special girl."

Suddenly excited that she could now relate to this somewhat strange conversation, Susannah piped up, "I know. She's the happiest little angel in the world. Isn't that what you said Daddy use to call her? His little angel?"

Mom smiled, but it was full of sadness. Susannah could feel the heaviness from it soak into her own body.

Mix, stir, mix.

"That's right. That's what Daddy used to call her. And there's a good reason for that."

"I know that too!" Susannah was proud to have the answers for a change. "He called her his angel because she loves God so much. Like how she smiles so big every time you sing her hymns. Hey, I have an idea. When she wakes up, maybe you can play the piano and we'll have a singalong."

Mom sighed. "Maybe, but right now your sister needs her rest. That's what I'm trying to tell you."

There it was. That heaviness again.

Stir, stir, mix.

"Kitty's not as strong as you are. That's why she takes extra naps each day and why she drinks her special formula instead of having big-girl food like you."

Susannah frowned. "I thought she just liked it better." She glanced up at Mom and then back at the bowl.

Mix, mix, mix.

Mom rubbed Susannah's back. "Kitty's such a special little angel she's not going to be able to walk or go to gymnastics or eat cookies like you do."

"Well, I know that. I'm just talking about later once she gets bigger and can do those things then. Won't it be fun?"

Mom let out a little cough. What had Susannah said wrong?

Mom was still rubbing her back as if she could erase the stains of Susannah's misspoken words. "Your sister isn't ever going to be big enough. She's always going to need someone to help her. She's always going to need someone to take care of her."

Susannah felt the heaviness surrounding her, not the heaviness of Mom's words but of her entire being. Her mom was tired. For the first time in her life, Susannah realized that.

Mom isn't as strong as she looks.

"It's ok, Mom. When I'm big enough I'll help you take care of Kitty."

She thought she was doing the right thing. Her promise was supposed to make Mom proud, but instead she turned and walked slowly out of the kitchen. Mom went into the bedroom, but even shutting the door and running the shower water wasn't enough to muffle the sound of her stifled sobs.

CHAPTER 14

Scott did his best to engage in the conversation around Carl and Sandy's table, but his mind kept snapping back to Susannah like the magnetic pull of a compass momentarily shaken off balance. Like the victim of some animistic curse, he was destined to relive that last phone call of theirs with perfect clarity.

"We can never be together." Five words. So final. Spoken with such tenderness, a tenderness that made the truth of her statement even harder to endure.

Never be together ...

He'd tried to change her mind. "Don't say that. Give yourself time to grieve. Let me walk through the mourning with you."

"I can't," she whispered, as if her soul was terrified of him, afraid of the attraction they'd felt for one another from so early on in their relationship. What was she scared of? Did she think he possessed the ability to hurt her?

"This is about Kitty, isn't it?" He tried not to sound

angry. Whenever he replayed the conversation, he chided himself for letting his passion get in the way of his clear thinking. Rational. He should have been rational.

"I made my mom a promise."

This wasn't happening. After ten years serving God overseas, he'd finally found a woman he wanted to call his wife. Finally found a woman who wasn't just willing but excited to travel the world with him, sharing the gospel, advancing the kingdom of God. They'd taken things slowly. At least it had felt slow to him. They'd prayed. Scott had humbled himself before Pastor Carl to ask for his advice, and Susannah had kept her mom filled in about their relationship from its earliest stages. It wasn't like they were sneaking around behind anyone's back or acting shamefully.

All they wanted to do was serve the Lord together. How could God ask them to give that up?

"She needs me." Susannah's voice was heavy with both sadness and conviction. She was such a demure, quiet-natured soul, but there were two things always guaranteed to stir up her passion — her zeal for world missions and her devotion to her sister.

Scott had heard so much about Kitty it was like he had already met her. Knew her smile. Understood the basic signs she used to communicate. Could probably talk with a doctor or nurse and fill them in on the basics of Kitty's medical history, from her preterm delivery when Susannah was only a toddler to the medical tests that eventually led to the diagnosis.

Scott had only known one other person with cerebral palsy. In sixth grade, one of his electives was as a volunteer buddy for another student. Zack had been in a wheelchair for as long as Scott could remember, had been nonverbal that whole time too, but he loved to laugh and listen to people talk about sports. For an entire semester, Scott's job was to spend forty-five minutes every day after lunch playing in the gym with Zack, placing the ball in his rigid hands and then shooting it toward the basket, congratulating him every time the ball came close to the rim.

He'd actually thought about Zack quite a bit last fall when he was still planning to visit Susannah and meet her family. He wanted to make sure he included Kitty in his discussions — it was a pet peeve of Susannah's when people ignored her sister or talked about her as if she weren't there — but he also didn't want to overdo it, make it look like he was trying too hard.

Turned out he didn't need to worry about any of that since Susannah was purging him out of her life. "I told my mom that when she died, I'd take care of Kitty."

"Let me move out there. We'll take care of her together." What else could he say? Even as he'd pleaded with her on the phone, he'd held the tiny ring in his hand, the ring he'd expected to give her when he flew out to Washington.

"I would never ask you to do that." Her voice was a mixture of shock and pain, as if he'd slapped her and then laughed in her face.

"You don't have to ask. I'm volunteering." Even as he said the words, he was trying to figure out how feasible it would be for him to continue working for Kingdom Builders from Washington. Just about every aspect of his job could theoretically be done remotely. The three-hour time difference would be the biggest complication, but Scott would rather learn to forgo sleep altogether than rip Susannah out of his heart.

"God's called you to the mission field," she reminded him. "And I can't go there with you."

"We'll make it work." Did she have any idea that he'd already bought her an engagement ring? Did she know that all the traveling in the world couldn't compare to life with her?

"I don't want to be a stumbling block to you. I don't want to keep you from your calling."

"But what about your calling?" He heard the intensity in

his voice and tried to soften it. "What about your heart for mission work?"

Her voice was steady and resolute. "It's a matter of priorities. *If someone does not provide for his own family, he has denied the faith and is worse than an unbeliever.*"

"You don't have to quote Scripture to me." Now he really was angry. Not at her, but at the situation. At her mom for dying. At God for bringing them together just to split them apart. At himself for not having found a way to make it to Washington sooner.

"I'm sorry, Scott." The words were so soft, he could hardly hear them.

"Please don't do this." He hated to sound so whiney. Like a little toddler throwing a fit because he didn't get his way. "Please. You don't understand how much I need you. I know you're trying to protect your heart here, and I respect that. I really do. But I love you. You don't have to say it back to me. You don't have to do anything except listen. But I love you. I want to spend the rest of my life with you."

He glanced at the ring that looked so delicate between his thumb and finger.

"A few weeks ago, I went out and bought you a ..." He stopped himself. Should he tell her? Would it just make matters worse? The words fell off his lips, carried on by inertia and no actual force of their own. "I bought you a ring."

She didn't reply. He wondered if she understood the gravity of what he'd just spoken.

"I want you to be my wife."

Silence. He checked his cell to make sure he hadn't gotten disconnected.

"Do you need more time to think about it?" he finally asked.

Still no response.

He sighed. "Just pray about it, and you can give me your answer later, all right? I know your sister needs you, and I would never ask you to turn your back on her. But I know that God's brought us together. The more I pray about it, the more convinced I am. We'll find a way to make it work. I know we will. Just please pray about it."

"Ok," she promised. "I will."

It was the last time he heard her voice.

CHAPTER 15

Susannah fidgeted with the strap of her purse. She had to get home. Kitty was supposed to eat her lunch at noon sharp. Any later, and she wouldn't tolerate her three o'clock snack.

It was nice of Derek to watch Kitty Sunday mornings, but Susannah couldn't depend indefinitely on her stepdad's generosity. Derek had only been part of the family for a few months. He liked Kitty, or at least that's what he told Susannah's mom, but he wasn't invested like Susannah was. For Derek, Kitty was part of the package if he wanted to marry her mom. For Susannah, her sister was now her calling, her ministry. Susannah's mission field, which she had at one point imagined to be the entire world, was now confined to a ten-by-fifteen bedroom.

The only thing I don't understand, God, is why you gave me all those desires to become a missionary if you weren't ever going to open those doors for me.

It wasn't like the global church was overrun by young men and women begging to be sent out to the mission field.

77

When Susannah was so willing, why would God bar the way?

Please forgive me for my lack of faith. Help me to focus on all the good things you've done in my life, all the ways you've provided for me.

Her mom's small life insurance plus Kitty's regular disability payments were enough so Susannah could move out of Derek's house and back into her mom's old place, which hadn't even been rented out yet. Susannah quit her job at Winter Grove and committed herself to caring for Kitty full-time. Her stepdad stopped by for a few hours Sunday mornings so she could go to church, and he dropped off groceries once a week, but when you've only been married for a few months before your wife dies, how long can you be expected to stay involved in the life of her disabled adult daughter?

Derek was a nice guy. Susannah had no complaints about him, but she knew that he wouldn't stick around forever. He was healthy, good-looking, stable, and eventually he would move on with his life. She couldn't begrudge him that. But she couldn't count on him indefinitely either. For all practical purposes, it was just her and her sister.

It had been hard to break up with Scott, or whatever you want to call what she did when she wrote him that last email.

She knew she'd hurt him, but what other choice was there? Scott would have given up anything for her. She realized that as soon as he mentioned moving to Washington. She wouldn't be responsible for making him drop out of his missionary work. She wouldn't put that kind of obstacle in his way.

When he told her about the ring, said that he was ready to propose to her, she'd faltered, but only for a second. The instant her mom died, any future Susannah and Scott may have tried to make for themselves became an impossibility.

An impossibility because Susannah could never leave her sister's side. She felt guilty enough for taking two hours off every Sunday so she could go to church. She could never leave the country or travel around the world.

She could never leave Orchard Grove.

Any scenario that Scott might suggest — and he dreamed up quite a few before she said goodbye — would have been just as unattainable. What if they got together, what if they were married? Would Scott keep his job and travel the world while Susannah stayed home with Kitty? What kind of wife could she be to him?

And even worse — what if he gave up his mission work? What if he decided to move to Orchard Grove, settle down, and play house with Susannah and Kitty? Then Susannah would be responsible before God for distracting a capable, willing missionary from his calling.

She couldn't.

She wouldn't.

God, I sacrificed him to you, and I'm trying hard to remember that you are enough for me. But I miss him so much. My spirit is willing, but my flesh is so weak. Please send me a little bit of encouragement today.

She glanced up at Grandma Lucy, and their eyes met. An electric jolt zapped Susannah's heart.

"What God has opened, no man will shut." Grandma Lucy didn't take her eyes off Susannah. "What God has ordained, no plans will thwart. *'Do I bring to the moment of birth and not give delivery?' says the LORD. 'Do I close up the womb when I bring to delivery?' says your God.*"

Power tugged at Susannah's spirit. Heaviness and warmth wrapped around her shoulders like a mantle. Conviction rose in her soul even as Grandma Lucy's voice increased in intensity.

"He is the God who finishes what he begins. He is the God who brings it to completion. He doesn't carry you to the moment of destiny and desert you there. He doesn't place a calling on your life and fail to bring it to pass. He will never abandon you or forsake you. Just like for the Israelites, it will be said of you that not one of all the LORD's good promises failed. Each and every one came to pass."

The words were like a tailwind that could whisk Susannah up and carry her away, straight off to paradise if she could hold onto them long enough. The warmth surrounding her turned into burning heat, the initial quickening in her spirit giving way to the undeniable presence of her glorious Savior. Wrapped in his grace, surrounded on all sides by his glory, her soul sang his praises even as her ears echoed with Grandma Lucy's words: *Not one of all the LORD's good promises failed. Each and every one came to pass.*

After a few more words, Grandma Lucy handed Pastor Greg back the mic, but the presence of God continued to encase Susannah's entire being. Here was love. Here was power.

The tears that streaked down her cheeks were just as hot as the burning passion and searing loss that invaded her soul.

CHAPTER 16

"Hey, Mr. Scott?" Woong plopped onto the couch and wiped ketchup stains off his face with the back of his hand. "You know what I'm wondering?"

Scott felt so relaxed even though he knew he had to get back to his apartment soon. Carl was famous for his Sunday afternoon naps, and Scott didn't want to impose on his family's hospitality more than he already had.

"No," he answered Woong. "What?"

"What I'm wondering is how come God sends out tapestries in the first place."

Scott tried to make sense of the question. The Lindgrens had adopted Woong from a South Korean orphanage, and even though there wasn't a trace of an accent to his English, he still got his words confused every once in a while. "Tapestries?"

"Yeah. You know, people who travel all over to Africa and Alaska and stuff and nonsense like that to teach them folks who never asked Jesus into their hearts how to do it right."

82

Scott chuckled. "They're called missionaries."

Woong frowned and cocked his head to the side. "Isn't that what I said? Why's God have people do that?"

Scott was about to tell Woong about the great commission, Jesus' last command to his disciples before he was taken up to heaven, but Woong still had more questions.

"Here's what I mean. Dad says that God already knows who's going to heaven and who isn't. I even heard him talk about it one Sunday. There was some sort of fancy word for it. The doctor of electives, I think he called it, or something close to it."

Before Scott could offer any corrections, Woong continued.

"And here's what I was thinking. Let's say my dad's right, which I know he is on account of him being a pastor and stuff and nonsense like that. So that means God already knows which folks are on their way to heaven and which folks have to spend forever in the other place. Now what I'm wanting to know is why people like you bother going out and being tapestries since God's already got his mind made up."

Scott stared at Woong, wondering how to simplify a debate that had made waves in the Christian church for centuries. "Well," he began, not because he knew what he was going to say next but because he figured he had to start somewhere. "The important thing to remember when we talk about the Lord is that ..."

"Woong, honey," Sandy called from the kitchen, "I need you to clear those dishes off the table and gave Mr. Scott a chance to relax, ok, baby?"

Woong pouted. "I'm not a baby," he grumbled and slid off the couch.

Carl came down the hall after taking off his tie. He lowered himself into the chair across from Scott with a groan. "I'm getting too old for this."

From the dining room, Woong asked his mom questions which she answered patiently as she loaded up the dishwasher. Scott was always impressed when he came to the Lindgrens' home. There was a peacefulness here, a kind of calm that he couldn't quite explain. He wasn't sure if it was a result of Sandy's homemaking skills, maybe all the framed Bible verses she'd put up on the walls, or the love that radiated from this couple who'd spent their lives raising foster kids, adopted kids, biological kids, and grandkids.

All he knew was that he felt more at peace here than he did anywhere else on the globe. And no matter how far away God called him in the future, it would be nice to have a place like this waiting for him upon his return.

A place to call home.

CHAPTER 17

Susannah wrapped her winter coat around herself and braced for the blast of wet snow as she stepped out the doors of Orchard Grove Bible Church. She kept her head down to protect her face from the biting wind and made her way to the car.

"Susannah! Hold up a minute."

She recognized the voice. Didn't want to turn around, but she couldn't be rude. She conjured up a smile. "Hi, Ricky."

He waved his hand in greeting even though he was now only two feet away. "Hey, what're you doing?"

Susannah let go of the handle of her car. "Just heading home. It's past Kitty's lunchtime."

Ricky shuffled from one foot to the other and then stamped both of them in the snow. "Yeah, I guess that's what happens when Grandma Lucy closes in prayer, huh?" He let out a nervous chuckle.

"I guess so," Susannah answered. She and Ricky Fields had known each other from the time they were both wearing diapers and drooling on plastic rattles in the Orchard Grove nursery. In addition to attending the same church, they often found themselves enrolled in the same co-op classes. In a moment of both indecisiveness and pity, Susannah had even agreed to be Ricky's date to the homeschool prom their junior year.

The snow was so heavy, it was falling down the back of Susannah's neck. She raised the fur-lined hood of her coat.

"Nice jacket." Ricky reached out as if he wanted to touch it then pulled his hand away. "I don't remember you wearing it before."

"It was my mom's," Susannah answered and watched Ricky's face melt into a puddle of mortification.

"I'm so sorry," he gasped. "I shouldn't have said anything. I should have known."

"How could you?" Susannah tried to offer a smile. "Don't worry about it."

"No, I feel terrible now. I'm always doing that, saying things at the worst possible times. I wasn't trying to make you sad. Honest I wasn't."

Susannah didn't bother to mention that she hadn't been feeling any worse than normal until he started making such a big deal about it.

"Let me make it up to you," he pleaded. "What can I do?

Can I drive you home? Walk you back to church? Do you need a cup of tea?"

Susannah had to smile at his earnestness if nothing else. "I'm fine. Really. It's just a coat."

Ricky's face wrinkled up. Susannah might have tried harder to convince him there wasn't any reason to feel bad, but she was already late. "I'm sorry," she apologized, even though she couldn't be sure what for. "I have to go now. Good to see you."

He shuffled again, a little bounce from one leg to the other, widening his footprint in the snow. "Ok, well, you know you can call me if you need anything, right? I've told you that before, and you haven't forgotten?"

She smiled. "I haven't forgotten. Thank you." She opened the door. "Please don't be upset. You didn't say anything wrong."

His face lit up as she lowered herself into the driver's seat. He stood there smiling and waving goodbye as Susannah put the car into reverse, wondering how long it would take before everyone around her stopped acting like she would break any minute.

How long it would take before everyone around her could simply forget.

CHAPTER 18

"Well, son." Carl clasped Scott on the shoulder. "You know we love having you over, and I hate to say it, but that Sunday nap of mine isn't going to take itself."

"You know what I'm wondering?" Woong asked from the corner where he'd been playing with some Legos.

His mom leaned down and whispered, "Not right now, baby."

Woong stuck out his lower lip. "I'm not a baby."

Scott stood and accepted Sandy's warm hug. "Thank you so much for the delicious lunch. It's always so nice spending time with you and your family."

Sandy smiled brightly as she pulled away. "You know you're welcome here anytime."

Carl extended his hand for a shake. "Anytime other than late Sunday afternoon," he added with a broad grin.

Scott smiled back. "Well, enjoy your nap. Thanks again for the encouraging sermon and a great time together afterward."

"You'll hafta come back soon." Woong glanced up from his Lego Avenger set. "'Cause I was reading my geometry book the other day, and they said there are these people who all live together on one big island, except they're the kind of people who don't wear much clothes, and when they get mad at each other and go to war, they actually eat each other right up, and when we were reading that Mom said you know a guy who printed a Bible for folks like that, and I wanted to ask you about it except I forgot until just now."

Scott stared perplexed until Sandy explained, "We've been reading Don Richardson."

"Now I get it. I was wondering what kind of geometry lessons he was getting," he added with a smile.

The Lindgrens lived a few blocks away from the nearest bus stop, and Scott was happy to walk. Enjoyed the quiet. He wondered what Susannah would think of Woong. Pictured how perfectly she and Sandy would get along. Wondered how different life might have been if God had kept Susannah in his life for good.

CHAPTER 19

No matter how hurried she felt, no matter how upset she was to be so late, Susannah had to drive slowly on account of the snow, which turned the Orchard Grove roads into nothing more than black sheets of ice.

Something Grandma Lucy had said at the end of her prayer time rang through Susannah's mind like the clanging bells in the church's Easter bell choir.

What God has opened, no man will shut.

It sounded so biblical. So true. How could God's plans ever be thwarted?

But was there more to it than that? Of course, God had a plan for every believer's life, but what about those who lived in open rebellion to him? What about those like Jonah who completely disobeyed? If Jonah hadn't repented and returned to Nineveh, would God have destroyed the city right then? Or would he have raised up another more willing prophet to spread his message?

God is omnipotent. All-powerful. Is it possible for his

90

plans not to succeed?

Not one of all the LORD's good promises failed. Each and every one came to pass.

Susannah's thoughts swirled as chaotically as the snowflakes falling from the sky, dancing and descending with no discernible purpose or sense of order.

Each and every one came to pass.

Of course, there were promises in the Bible, promises that Susannah knew to be true. Jesus would one day return. He would establish his kingdom on earth, a kingdom without pain or mourning or sin. A kingdom where every man, woman, and child would worship the true King in all his splendor.

And there were promises for her own life too. Promises that God would wipe away all her tears. She believed it to be true even though for now she'd only caught short glimpses, ephemeral flashes of the comfort that would one day soothe over all her wounds.

He is the God who finishes what he begins, Grandma Lucy had said. *He is the God who brings it to completion.*

There were so many things Susannah couldn't understand. Why God would give her such a passion for the mission field only to stand by idly when her mother's death and her sister's disability trapped her in Orchard Grove for the rest of her life.

Why God would bring such a strong, confident man like Scott into her life only to ask her to give him up after everything that happened. To sacrifice her own happiness and future in order to care for the sister she loved.

More than anything, she was afraid that one day all this sorrow, all these disappointments would make her bitter. She had worked with caregivers like that at the assisted living home, people who twenty or thirty years ago might have been compassionate and gentle, but who got tired and burnt out and jaded by the difficulties of their jobs.

Who resented the patients entrusted into their care.

Dear God, please keep my heart from growing hard. Please give me the patience and tenderness I need. Please help me to love Kitty as well as Mom did. I can't do any of this without you, Lord.

The snow continued to fall as Susannah pulled her car into the driveway. She didn't know how to protect her own heart in the face of the sorrows and disappointments. She didn't know how to make sense of her grief, grief over burying her mother and losing Scott.

But she was convinced that God had promised to never leave her or forsake her. As she made her way up the slushy, icy walkway to her front door, she knew that he would have to be enough.

CHAPTER 20

Riding the bus back to his apartment, Scott pulled out his phone. He'd been so good lately about not checking his messages, wondering every five or ten minutes if he might have an email from her. But even though he knew there wouldn't be one today, his heart raced as he opened his inbox.

A few messages from coworkers, but nothing that couldn't wait until he got into the office tomorrow. Two emails from missions' news websites, which he saved to read later.

And that was all.

The disappointment was as real and as poignant as it had been four months ago.

He stared at his inbox, knowing he should close it. Knowing nothing good could come from keeping it open. Knowing that if he let himself dwell in the past, he'd be useless for the rest of the day.

He tapped the button anyway.

Susannah Peters.

He'd given her emails a folder of their own. It was the only way to keep his inbox even slightly decluttered. There were over a thousand by now. Some were long and would fill three or four pages if he printed them up. Others were nothing more than a quick Bible verse or word of encouragement she wanted to share with him in the middle of a busy day.

He stared at the subject lines, remembering the sweet thrill that always accompanied her notes when they were together.

No, not together in the traditional sense. He'd never held her hand. Never brushed his lips against her temple or run his fingers through her hair. Because of her mom's strict rules and the bandwidth issues in Orchard Grove, they'd never even chatted in a video call. The only reason he knew what it was like to stare into her eyes was because of the hours he spent gazing at the one photograph she'd sent him.

Hopeful hours. Hours of prayerful longing and physical yearning.

Wasted, all of them.

The bus jostled, and Scott's finger accidentally tapped his screen. Or maybe it wasn't quite as accidental as he wanted to believe, and then he was peering into the documented history of both the deepest joy and sharpest pain of his adult life.

The documented history of all the exhilaration and excitement and thrills as well as the heartache from which there was no escape.

CHAPTER 21

Susannah wiped her boots on the welcome mat and slipped them off as she entered the house. "Kitty, I'm back!" she called.

God, please forgive me for being abrupt with Ricky in the parking lot and for being impatient to get home. Thank you for bringing me here safely. Please make Kitty's stomach able to handle lunch a little late without it messing up her snack time later on.

Derek glanced up from the couch as she passed. "How was church?"

She jumped into her apology without answering his question directly. "I'm sorry I wasn't back sooner. Service got out late, and the roads are pretty icy."

Derek held his book in his hands. "Don't worry about it. She did fine. She's just in there listening to her tapes."

Years earlier, Susannah's mom had saved up enough money to buy the first ten years of the *Adventures in Odyssey* radio dramas on cassette. Since she refused to bring a TV into the home, the episodes were Kitty's primary mode of entertainment when everyone else was busy. When their tape player broke a while back, Derek had to order a new one online since none of the local stores sold them anymore.

Susannah hurried into the back room, mentally calculating how she would adjust her sister's feeding schedule now that lunch was delayed. With a digestive system as fickle as Kitty's, the ramifications from even a fifteen-minute deviation from normal could last for days.

Dear God, please help it not get too bad this time.

She felt guilty for wasting God's time on these sorts of prayers. With all the lost and hurting in the world, with all the people destined to die in their sins and suffer for eternity, why should God care about her sister's eating habits?

Of course he cared, but that still didn't keep Susannah from feeling guilty.

Kitty was lying down when Susannah came into the room. "Oh, so you're going to keep your head to the wall and not say hi. Is that it?" She kept her voice playful and walked up to her sister's bedside. "You better watch out, or I might have to tickle you while I'm rubbing the kinks out of your back."

She didn't even have to touch her sister. Just hearing the

word *tickle* was enough to make Kitty snort even though she tried to hide her amusement.

"I can see you trying not to laugh over there." Susannah reached out, but Kitty flinched. "I'm not tickling you," she told her sister. "That was just a joke. But let's give you a little backrub before we get you ready for lunch."

It was Susannah's mom who discovered that Kitty could handle her bottle of formula better after a massage. That simple discovery had helped Kitty gain fifteen pounds and kept her from needing a permanent feeding tube.

With hands and fingers made strong from years of practice, Susannah probed out Kitty's tight muscles and addressed them one by one. "Everybody missed you in church, you know. That new pastor, the one I told you about with the pretty wife from California, he said to me. 'Susannah, when do I get to meet that gorgeous sister of yours I've been hearing so much about? I'm beginning to think you made up a story about her just to tease me.'"

Kitty's body tensed up as she let out a jerky laugh. Susannah kept kneading the knots out of her sister's shoulders.

"You think it's funny, but now I'm about to get in trouble with the pastor because he thinks I'm lying. I told him I'd bring him a picture of you, but he said, 'Well, anyone can find a picture online these days. How do I know you're not going to find a picture of someone else's sister and bring it to me instead?'"

Derek cleared his throat in the entrance. "Got to run, you two, or I'll miss the afternoon service."

"Thanks again for coming by," Susannah said.

"No prob." Derek winked. "See you later, kiddo." Susannah wasn't sure if he was talking to her or her sister.

"Thanks for visiting!" she called out in that same cheerful voice she always used around Kitty and then went back to her story about the pastor. "So anyway, Pastor Greg said, 'If you don't bring your sister to the Christmas Eve service, I'm going to assume that you just made up the entire story, and I'm going to be really mad at you.' So I said, 'Oh, please don't, Pastor. Kitty wants to come to church. She really does, but you know how much Mom worries about her. She doesn't want her going out in the winter when she could catch a cold. Or what if we slipped on the ice while we were helping her into the car?' So he agreed that he wouldn't mind waiting to meet you. 'Your mom's such a wise woman,' he said."

It always pained Susannah to talk about their mother in the present tense like that. She had tried explaining it to Kitty before, but there was something about her sister's pure and innocent mind that couldn't grasp the finality of death. The few times it did sink in, Kitty either threw up or refused to eat, and then she still forgot about it the following day. It was Derek who finally told Susannah she may as well talk to Kitty as if her mother were still alive. Susannah hated the hint of deceit, but in the end decided maybe her stepdad was right.

Kitty was so empathetic, and her gut was so connected to her emotional life, that Susannah knew she shouldn't dwell on these disturbing memories, especially not before lunchtime. She smiled and infused as much cheer into her voice as possible and said, "I saw your boyfriend today."

Kitty displayed her pleasure by kicking the mattress with her one good leg. It was no secret that Kitty's crush on Ricky Fields extended at least as far back as the junior prom when he'd been Susannah's date.

Susannah was glad to see her sister so happy. "He asked how you're doing, you know. Wants to know if you still keep his picture on your nightstand."

Two more kicks with her leg, one right after the other.

Susannah sighed melodramatically. "Imagine how sad he was when I told him you'd forgotten all about that picture."

Kitty thrashed her head to the side. Even though her sister was grinning broadly, Susannah didn't have the heart to carry on the teasing further. "I'm joking. He knows how special that picture is to you. Do you want to look at it after I help you sit up?"

Another kick. This one calmer.

"Ok." After working out the worst of Kitty's knots and gently turning her over, Susannah raised the head of the bed so she was sitting up. "Do you want lunch here or in the kitchen?"

Kitty slapped her thigh with her right hand. "Here?" Susannah guessed.

Two slaps now. Kitty threw her head to the side.

"Oh. You want to see the picture? I told you that's what we'd do first."

Kick.

Susannah reached for the framed photograph. "All right, here's your Prince Charming. Isn't he handsome?"

Kitty grunted in agreement, and Susannah stared at the image. While she'd done her best to endure Ricky Field's awkward mannerisms and sweaty hands at the homeschool prom, her mom had noticed Kitty's dejected mood and decided to give her a prom of her own. She dressed Kitty up in a hot-pink bridesmaid's gown from decades earlier, poofy bows and all. When Ricky brought Susannah home for her ten o'clock curfew, Mom and Kitty were in the living room listening to *My Girl*, one of the only secular songs the Peters owned.

"You look beautiful, Kitty," Ricky had said, bowing slightly toward her wheelchair, and for the first time Susannah thought she might have liked to kiss him if she had permission to.

Without waiting for any prompting, he walked up to Susannah's mom and asked, "May I dance with your daughter?"

Her mom's expression was hard to read when she answered, "You'll have to ask her yourself. Kitty, do you want to dance with this boy?"

One kick. Grin. Another kick.

"That means yes," Susannah explained, wondering how in the world her date expected to dance with her sister, but apparently Ricky's somewhat clunky moves were well suited for the occasion.

"*I got sunshine on a cloudy day,*" he sang, apparently forgetting he'd spent the entire night with Susannah completely tongue-tied. At first, by the way he pushed Kitty back and forth in her wheelchair, she may as well have been a vacuum cleaner, but by the second chorus, he grew a little more savvy, even tipping her back on her wheels for a dip and making her mom squeal in fear.

Kitty howled — which really is the literal way to describe it — with delight, and after the last chorus died out, her mom ran to grab the camera to capture the moment forever. In the photo, Ricky has taken Kitty's good hand and is leaning over it like he's about to give her a kiss. There's something charming in his expression Susannah recognized even as she joked around with her sister.

"I still can't believe you stole my date from me that night."

A kick and a wide grin.

"That's probably why you made Mom get you all dressed up, huh? You knew that one look at you and Ricky Fields couldn't resist, right?"

Grinning even wider.

Susannah set the picture back on her sister's nightstand and gave her a gentle kiss on the cheek. "Come on, let's get you some lunch."

CHAPTER 22

January 7

Dear Scott, How are you? My name is Susannah Peters. Buck, the Mobilization Director from Kingdom Builders, forwarded your e-mail address to me. I hope you don't mind my taking the liberty to write you. My heart's desire is to serve God internationally. When I first heard God's call to missions, I kept expecting and asking him to tell me where I was supposed to go, but the more I kept praying, the more I realized there wasn't one specific area of the earth I felt more called to than any other. The season of harvest is now, but the harvest is everywhere!

That's why I was so excited to learn about the Kingdom Builders ministry. I'd never thought before about the need for an agency that ministers to missionaries, but I think it's so neat that you guys aren't focused on one geographic area but serve God all throughout the world by strengthening those he's raised up to spread the gospel to the distant shores.

I looked up some information about the Kingdom Builders summer internship program, and as soon as I read the description of the program I realized it's exactly the kind of opportunity I've been looking for to "test out God's call" on my life and see if full-time missions really is his will for me. So I guess I'm writing both to hear a little bit more about the summer program as well as find out what's necessary to begin the application process. I know my mom will have a lot of questions about it too because I've never left the country before.

I suppose that's it, but I do want to let you know again how excited I am about the work Kingdom Builders is doing to bring God's glory to the nations! I will be praying for you and your ministry.

Wishing you God's richest blessings,
Susannah Peters

CHAPTER 23

Lying in bed that night, Susannah thought over her day. *Lord, I didn't miss Scott this afternoon as much as I sometimes do. I'm really thankful for that.*

It was one of the many blessings of being her sister's only caretaker. Susannah was so busy at home that she didn't have time to brood.

I'm sorry for teasing Kitty about Ricky. You know I don't mean anything by it, and it makes her so happy, but maybe it's wrong of me to treat her like that. Make her think Ricky likes her. Get her hopes up.

Susannah knew all about shattered hopes.

Thank you for a good church service today. I'm sorry I didn't pay more attention. And thank you that Derek's willing to watch Kitty Sunday mornings. Please bless him for all the kindnesses he shows us both.

Susannah didn't expect any sort of typical father-daughter relationship with her stepdad, but she was grateful he'd stayed involved in her life. None of her mom's church friends had taken that kind of interest in her and her sister.

Lord, I'm sure there are many other things I'm forgetting to thank you for and even more that I'm forgetting to confess. I'm just so tired.

She strained her ears, listening for her sister's breathing, which was something between a snore and the sound of a coffee maker percolating.

God, I love her so much. Thank you for allowing me to take care of Kitty. Thank you for allowing me to fulfill my promise to Mom.

She didn't know if people could look down from heaven once they'd died. She'd never actually heard a pastor preach against that kind of theology, but she guessed it wouldn't line up with the typical stoic orthodoxy of a church like Orchard Grove.

If she's up there, God, I hope you'll tell her not to worry about us.

That's nearly all Mom did while she was alive. Care for Kitty and worry about her girls. Worry about Susannah's love life, about Kitty's digestion. Fret over leaving Kitty without a caretaker. Of course, nobody expected her to die so young, but Susannah and her mother had already discussed the issue multiple times.

"I'll take care of Kitty. No matter where I am, I'll come

home and look after her once you're gone."

"I don't want to put that kind of burden on you. Only God knows where you'll be at that point in time, where you'll be serving him."

Susannah had silenced her mother's protests. "When God takes you home, I'll just take that as my message from him that he's calling me back to Orchard Grove, back to the family I love so much."

God, I know that not even a sparrow falls to the ground apart from your will. You knew about that car accident long before it ever happened. You knew exactly when Mom was going to leave us, and I'm so glad you took her quickly. No suffering. But couldn't you have waited? Even a few weeks …

Would things have been different if Scott had come to visit first? He said he'd picked out a ring. If she'd been engaged when her mother died, would that have changed things? Betrothals today weren't like in Bible times. Calling off an engagement wasn't the same thing as getting a divorce, but there was still a promise there. You'd given someone your word.

If Scott had flown out to Orchard Grove, if he'd put that ring on Susannah's finger, would Susannah have considered herself bound to him from then on?

Would she have felt the freedom from God to marry him, even if it meant pulling him away from the mission field?

God, it's such a waste of time to think about all these questions. Please calm my racing mind.

She tried to remember the songs she'd sung in church that morning. Mentally played through each one. Keep her mind focused on things above, just like the Bible verse said.

But every so often she'd realize that she'd switched songs without knowing it.

Every so often, the chorus of *My Girl* floated through her head, except now instead of seeing her sister dancing with the gangly, awkward boy from youth group, she imagined dancing with Scott to it on their wedding day.

CHAPTER 24

January 13

Hi, Scott. Wow, it was so fun talking to you over the weekend. Words can't express how thankful I am to you for taking time to answer my questions. I feel like I talked your ear off, and I'm really sorry for that. It's just hard to exaggerate what a blessing and a privilege it is to spend time in fellowship with somebody who's so passionate about spreading the Lord's glory throughout the earth.

I sometimes think about that day when God called me to the mission field. At the time, I felt really lonely. My mom was happy for me like I knew she would be. In fact, she showed me a picture I drew all the way back in kindergarten and wrote about how I wanted to be a "meshanarie" when I grew up, but everybody else just treated me like it was a phase. I remember for a while worrying that maybe it was, maybe it wasn't the Holy Spirit speaking to me at all. Maybe I was just getting caught up in the emotions of it.

Anyway, that was years ago, but what I really want to say is how refreshing it is to meet someone with a similar heart for the nations. I have to admit I'm nervous about submitting my application to Kingdom Builders. I know you told me not to worry about it, but the more I think about it the more I really, firmly believe that this is God's next step for me. The problem is it's a huge step. Mom's pretty worried. After our dad died when we were so young and with my sister being so fragile, I understand how she can be anxious. I only mention that because I've never actually been away from home for more than one or two nights here and there. Mom's totally behind me applying for the summer internship, especially after I passed on some of your answers to the questions she had (thank you so much for not freaking out about all of those), but I think it will be hard for us to be separated.

I'll probably feel guilty leaving Kitty too. I think about that a lot. But you didn't ask about my entire family history, so sorry about that! I don't know what got me so side-tracked. About your question for the pastoral reference, I called the church, and I guess they do have a fax machine, but it doesn't work all the time, so my pastor asked if you could email it to him. Thanks so much, not only for helping me out with this application and the seemingly endless questions my mom and I keep coming up with, but for being someone I can really talk to about missions. Orchard Grove's kind of a small community. There's no one else like that around here.

Blessings,
Susannah Peters

CHAPTER 25

"Good morning, sunshine," Susannah sang out as she bustled into Kitty's room. "Did you sleep well?"

Susannah's mom had defied just about every piece of medical advice by letting Kitty sleep on her stomach, where she seemed the most comfortable, and Susannah certainly wasn't one to change such a long-standing tradition. She perched on the side of her sister's bed and began massaging her back.

"How's my favorite sister doing today? Did you dream about Prince Charming?"

Kitty squirmed playfully beneath Susannah's touch.

"Did he dance the night away with you?"

More squirming.

"Did he sing you love songs? Did it sound like this?" Susannah hummed the first few lines of *My Girl*. It was too much excitement for Kitty, who kicked her legs three times and tried to slap her pillow.

"All right now," Susannah coaxed, "you've got to calm

down a little bit or you'll have a hard time with your breakfast. Let me work a little bit longer on your back. No, I'm not tickling, I'm just trying to get this muscle to relax a little bit. Then we'll get you in your chair. I have a really good idea. Let's eat breakfast in the dining room today."

Susannah was ashamed for how lax she'd gotten about her sister's mealtime routines. When Mom was alive, Kitty ate in the dining room unless she was sick, but Susannah could tell it was uncomfortable for her sister to shuffle in and out of the wheelchair, so she usually let Kitty decide where she wanted to eat. If she wasn't paying close attention, Kitty could go an entire day without getting out of bed. Even though Susannah was careful to turn her regularly so she wouldn't get bedsores, she knew her mom had the right idea about getting her sister out of her room.

It was easier in the summer, when the Orchard Grove heat conspired with their very sporadic air conditioning unit to force them out of doors, into the bright sunshine. Susannah couldn't even remember the last time Kitty had been outside.

Well, God, life isn't going exactly as I expected it, but I have so much to be grateful for. In spite of all that you've brought me through, even though I don't feel you right now, I know you're with me and Kitty both. You have given us so many blessings, and I'm forever thankful. Help me to keep my eyes on you today, and I know that everything is going to turn out just fine.

CHAPTER 26

February 2

Dear Scott,

Great news! Mom and Derek got engaged last night. It was really romantic. I kind of knew it was coming. He pulled me aside, not exactly to ask for my blessing, but he told me that he valued my opinion and wanted to know if I was comfortable with the timing or if I thought he and Mom were taking things too fast. It was really respectful of him, and I admired him a lot for that. It's not like I know him all that well, but it's taken my mom fifteen years to meet someone that she says is as godly and honorable as my dad was, and she's the best judge of character I know. So anyway, I knew he was going to pop the question, I just didn't know when. I figured it would be something pretty typical, you know, fancy dinner out or whatever. But he actually proposed at home. Kitty and I were both there, and even though he's not really trying to jump into our lives or take on some big

116

important role as a surrogate dad or anything, I thought it was a nice gesture.

Remember that picture I told you about that Kitty keeps on her nightstand, the one where she's in mom's old bridesmaid dress and she's dancing with that boy from our church? Derek knows how big of a crush she's got on him still. It's something we all like to joke about because it makes Kitty laugh so hard. What he did was look at the picture and asked Kitty about that night. He asked something like, "When that boy took your hand for the picture, was it like this?" And then he grabbed Mom and held her the same way.

Then he said, "And when he leaned over to kiss your hand, did he look into your eyes like this?" And that's what he did to Mom. I'm sure you get the idea.

So we all thought he was just being funny because the first time you hear Kitty laugh, all you want to do from that moment on is find more funny things to tell her. You heard her giggling when we put you on speaker phone the other evening, remember that? Anyway, I thought Derek was just having fun, but then all of a sudden he was on his knee, still holding Mom's hand, and that's when he asked her to marry him. I wish someone had thought to get the whole thing on camera because I can't remember a word he said. But it was really sweet and romantic, and obviously Mom told him yes.

So there's a wedding in her future!

I don't think it'll interfere at all with the internship this summer. They're looking into getting married in the early spring, so by the time the Kingdom Builders program starts, everyone should be settled in Derek's home and Kitty should be adjusted to her new surroundings. I actually feel better about leaving for the whole summer knowing that my mom will have someone else to help out with Kitty. I mean, Derek's at work all day, so it will still be Mom doing all the regular stuff, but at least she'll have someone to talk to at night and on the weekends.

I'd hate to think of her spending the whole summer in a big empty house taking care of Kitty all alone while I'm gone.

Anyway, they called me in for the evening shift at Winter Grove tonight, so I probably won't be able to talk to you until tomorrow evening. I just wanted to tell you the good news. Hope you're having a good day. Don't forget to let me know if sleeping with those onion slices in your socks helped with that sore throat or not. Mom swears by it.

Blessings,
Susannah

CHAPTER 27

Dear God, thank you so much for giving Kitty such a good morning. Thank you that she's been handling her food just fine even though yesterday's schedule got a little mixed up. Thank you for the way she takes these morning naps so I can have a little quiet time with you.

On days like these, Susannah would stop and think about her mother, think about how hard it would have been to be newly widowed with a baby as fragile as Kitty and a toddler to take care of on top of everything else. Susannah wished her mom was still alive so she could thank her for all the sacrifices she'd made for their family.

Sacrifices. There was that word again.

God, this weekend was hard. I thought about Scott more than I should have. The church service didn't help, either. Grandma Lucy's words really got me confused. You tell us in Scripture that you carry things on to completion, that you don't bring something to the point of delivery and then just let it miscarry, but what about the mission field? What about Scott?

119

I know I shouldn't always be questioning you. I should just calm down and trust that you've got it all under control, but it's hard to do. Mom's the one I would normally talk through all these things with, which makes it even harder. Maybe I shouldn't miss her as much as I do. Maybe her passing should just be a reminder to me to look forward to the day when we're all reunited in your glorious kingdom, but that's not so easy to do. I need your help.

Susannah stared at the open Bible in her lap. Several years ago, her mom had taught her a system for morning quiet times that she still used regularly. Giving thanks, confessing sins, then meditating on Scripture.

Today, Susannah was in Psalm 85.

"You, Lord, showed favor to your land; you restored the fortunes of Jacob. You forgave the iniquity of your people and covered all their sins. You set aside all your wrath and turned from your fierce anger."

Lord, you've forgiven me for so many things. My lack of faith, my doubts that you really had my good in mind when you took Mom home. Thank you so much for dying for me, for taking the punishment for all my sins, even the ones I haven't recognized yet.

"Restore us again, God our Savior, and put away your displeasure toward us. Will you be angry with us forever?

Will you prolong your anger through all generations? Will you not revive us again, that your people may rejoice in you? Show us your unfailing love, Lord, and grant us your salvation."

Restore. Susannah paused. Tried to think of a different way to describe it if she could.

Restore. God had taken so many things from her. Her mom. Her dreams of going on the mission field. Her relationship with Scott.

Restore. The word kept coming back to her. Was it possible?

God, only you know the future you have planned for me. Only you know if I'll ever find my way to serve you outside of Orchard Grove. Only you know if I'll ever meet someone else like Scott, someone with a passion for missions. I know that now wasn't the right time for those things, and I'm trying not to complain. I'm trying to give them up calmly and selflessly, but then you keep making it harder. You sent me to church to listen to Grandma Lucy talk about how you complete what you begin. You led me to the Psalm that talks about your perfect restoration when you yourself know that what I long for more than anything is for you to restore the joy I had when Mom was here and Scott and I were together and our plans were to serve you as full-time missionaries.

Right now, I don't even know what it would look like for you to restore any of those things, but since you've put that word in my heart, I'm going to ask you one more time.

Restore my joy. It doesn't matter to me how you do it. But come and restore my joy, and if it's your will, I pray that you would at least fulfill my dream of one day serving you on foreign soil.

CHAPTER 28

February 18

Dear Scott,

I just got home from Winter Grove and have to tell you what happened. You know how I've been a little impatient for God to bring me to the mission field? I think you more than anybody understands what it's like to have that longing and to always wonder if God's going to fulfill it or not.

So I hate to confess it, but I've been a little anxious, asking God what he's doing and not really trusting his plans or his timing, which are so perfect! Today, I was having a rough shift at work. It wasn't anything about the residents. If my entire job was just taking care of the elderly, I would be thrilled. But there's a lot of other stuff going on too, behind-the-scenes drama. My co-workers are really upset with the administration because they're changing up the overtime schedule. Anyway, that's all beside the point. The only reason I bring it up is because a lot of people today were upset and grumbling about the new policy, and I can't blame them. It doesn't make a huge difference to me as long as they keep on giving me Sundays off, but it's really inconvenient for some of the others.

But back to work. I was having a hard day because first everyone around me was upset about the policy, and second I just felt really impatient, more so than normal, to get onto the mission field. I know the Kingdom Builders summer program's only a few months away, and I'm so excited Mom agreed to let me go, but even that internship's not the full-time missionary work I feel called to.

So I was helping the residents get ready for breakfast, and in between rooms I was praying to God and asking him to give me a better perspective, and I thought about what you said the other night when we were talking, how every Christian should be in full-time ministry, no matter what their actual job is. And I know I've heard things like that before, but it really hit home today. So I asked myself, "How would my job look different if I was from another country and raised support to work here at Winter Grove?"

It really changed my outlook, and it really encouraged me to start to think of myself as a missionary right where I am. My mom always tells me, "Bloom where you're planted," which is kind of cute and clichéd, but it really makes sense.

I started to pray for more opportunities to share the gospel with the people around me, and there's this one resident who's been really difficult for me. Not difficult to get along with, I'm just talking like literally hard because he's at least a hundred pounds overweight and doesn't want to use a wheelchair, but he needs a lot of help getting places. And he doesn't talk, either. He's one of the sad ones who just seems trapped inside himself.

Anyway, I was taking him to the bathroom of all places, and I was thinking about Winter Grove as a mission field, and so I asked him if he knew about Jesus. And it was really awkward because he's so hard of hearing I had to shout in his ear. I'm not exaggerating, either, I was literally shouting, "Do you know who Jesus is and how he died to save you from your sins?"

And I'll never forget it, but as soon as I said that, he got totally lucid. No confusion or anything, and he looked at me and for the first time his eyes weren't glazed over. And he said, "I don't know him."

So I said (or shouted, really), "Do you want to?" And he looked right at me and nodded! I only got to talk to him for another minute or so because one of my co-workers came up then to pass out his meds, and then the glassy look was back and we never got another moment like that. But I'm praying for more breakthroughs for him, and I'd love for you to pray too. His name is Duke. He used to be a professional boxer. Can you believe that?

That's all for now, because I told Mom I'd help with Kitty's snack while she runs to the store. She's going to make her own wedding cake and is doing a practice run today!

Talk with you soon!

Blessings,

Susannah

ALANA TERRY

CHAPTER 29

"Come on, Kitty. Just another two sips, ok? Two sips and we can be done."

Susannah wiped her forehead. It was thirty-one degrees outside, but her pits were slimy with sweat.

She raised the formula bottle to her sister's lips. "Just a little more. You can do it."

Kitty made a move like she was about to gag.

"None of that now." Susannah sounded sterner than she'd intended. She wiped some of the dribbled formula off her sister's chin, trying to maintain a gentle touch that would conceal her impatience and irritation.

God, I know that in the grand scheme of things it really shouldn't matter whether it takes her ten minutes or an hour to drink this bottle, but can you please help her get through it a little faster?

The worst part was that Susannah's hurry was completely unfounded. It wasn't like she had anywhere to go. Derek would stop by later with a few bags of groceries,

127

Susannah would try to offer him twenty or forty dollars which he'd refuse, and that would be the extent of her interaction today with anyone else besides her sister.

Would things be different if she hadn't cut off all communication with Scott? Maybe. In the short term, it would be nice to have someone to talk to about her day. Another sound to listen to at night besides her sister's gurgled snoring.

But in the end, it was best to call things off when she did. With his heart on the mission field and Susannah stuck here in Orchard Grove, there was no way to pretend it was possible for them to forge a future together.

Better to cut him off now. Let the pain of losing him merge and morph into the grief over Mom's death. Like getting all four wisdom teeth pulled on the same day instead of dragging it out one or two at a time.

She and Scott could never be together. Their fate was sealed the moment Mom left home to buy that friendship bread starter. Even if Susannah hadn't broken up with him, even if they'd kept on talking for months or even years, it would only make their inevitable separation that much more unbearable.

God, I'm so glad you didn't allow us to meet face to face. All those disappointments where I couldn't understand why you wouldn't let us come together when we wanted … I'm sorry I didn't thank you for those things at the time. I see now that you were being gracious to us all along. That you were protecting me from falling even more in love with him because you knew it would make things that much harder now.

"Come on, Kitty," Susannah whined and tried to coax one more sip out of her sister. "You've got to drink a little more to stay strong and healthy."

If Susannah had inherited anything negative from her mother, it was her propensity to worry. Cold and flu season was the worst. Last spring, a lingering cough threatened to develop into pneumonia, and Kitty still hadn't recovered by the time Susannah was supposed to start her internship with Kingdom Builders.

Another example of God's intervention on her behalf.

Of course, she and Scott were already intimate at that point. Already talking about love and romance and an eventual engagement in spite of all of her mother's admonitions to take things slowly. Susannah had been disappointed when she couldn't spend the summer overseas like she'd planned. Still, through it all, she had smiled, thanked God she was able to spend extra time with her sister, whose strength returned steadily day by day, and she'd sent

Scott emails each evening to fill him in on Kitty's improving health.

There was no rush. She and Scott had all the time in the world. At least that's the lie she'd believed when life felt so full, the future so promising.

"Ok, last sip." She held the bottle up but didn't recognize Kitty's pre-gag warning signs in time to move out of the way. She tried not to grimace when hot formula and stomach acid spilled onto her.

"It's ok," she said, even though she was sure Kitty was paying more attention to her incriminating body language than her actual words. "It's ok," she repeated. "Let's get you cleaned up and go listen to an *Odyssey* together."

Susannah turned her back to her sister, forced down the annoying lump in her throat, and stifled a silent cry of frustration.

CHAPTER 30

February 27

Dear Scott,

I have so much to tell you but don't know how to express it. Maybe I'm afraid.

Your email yesterday really touched and encouraged me. I wanted you to know that before I said or did anything else. To think that you could feel so strongly about a girl you haven't even met face to face … I love how you told me it didn't even matter that you hadn't seen my picture yet. It made me feel so safe, like you were really here to get to know me. No ulterior motives. So thank you.

And thank you for being honest. I'm sure it must have been scary writing all that and not knowing how I'd respond, and then I'm sure it was hard waiting to hear back from me until now. I wasn't ignoring you. I just wanted to talk to my mom about it first, and she's been so busy with wedding plans, and Kitty's got the sniffles, which is probably nothing serious but always makes Mom nervous.

But I did finally find the right time to tell her about your email, so imagine my surprise when she said you'd actually called her! You could have told me that! She said that she was happy for me like I knew she would be, but she still wants me to be careful. Wants to make sure I'm not giving you my whole heart until we've met and she's gotten the chance to get to know you better and we're all convinced that this is the direction God is calling us to take. But she likes your idea and definition of courtship, how we wouldn't be just dating to have someone to be with, but we're really praying and trying to seek God's will to decide if we're supposed to spend our future together.

So the answer to your question (and sorry for taking so long to get there!) is yes, I would be honored to begin prayerfully considering if God has more in store for us than just a whole lot of emails and late nights on the phone!

I'm trying to be cautious like Mom said, but when you and I talked that very first time, and through all the emails and phone conversations since then, I've realized more and more that you are the kind of man I always pictured myself with. But I told myself I was being silly. I'm too young.

You've been all over the world. You've served so many places, been used by God in so many ways. What would you see in a girl like me?

That's why when I read your email, I didn't know how to react. Yes, I was surprised, but that doesn't mean I hadn't hoped for something like this. I'm just so overwhelmed right now. I'm like Job. I put my hands over my mouth and have no idea what to say.

I hope that my somewhat flustered reply doesn't hurt your feelings. The last thing I want is for you to believe your thoughts and emotions aren't reciprocated. But I'm so young, and my mom is truly the wisest woman I've ever met, and I'm trying to take her advice and keep my heart guarded.

The spirit is willing, as they say, but the flesh is weak.

I wish I could blindly trust my own intuition, which is to throw myself headfirst into this relationship, but I should listen to Mom and go slowly. Be patient with me. I've never fallen in love before. I know you understand.

I'll write more later. I hardly slept at all last night. Mom and I were talking past midnight, and I was up early with Kitty because of her stuffy nose. I just couldn't let another hour go by without writing you, without telling you how deeply honored I am that you would consider me, a girl you've never even met. I know there's so much more to talk about, so much more to pray about, but right now I'm just going to trust all that to God's timing and let you know how closely I hold you in my heart.

Blessings,
Your Susannah

CHAPTER 31

Susannah stared at her clock, trying to figure out how it could be 4:43 in the morning with the sun coming in her room.

She rubbed her eyes then jerked herself fully awake. What was going on? Had something happened to Kitty?

She grabbed her phone. 4:43. It didn't make sense.

Unless it was the afternoon. Had she fallen asleep while her sister napped?

"Kitty?" she called out, straining her ears for sounds of snoring. "You ok?"

No response. Not that she'd expected much.

She jumped out of bed, ignoring the dizzy spinning in her head and the groggy heaviness in her body. She plodded down the hall to Kitty's room. "You in there?"

Kitty was on her side, her back facing the door. How long had Susannah been sleeping? Nearly two hours? How could she have gotten that exhausted in the first place?

"Kitty?" she whispered, trying not to startle her sister. "Kitty?"

She touched her on the shoulder. No response.

Hurrying to the other side of the bed, she peered into her sister's face. "Kitty?"

A single, silent tear shined in the pre-dusk sunlight streaming in from the window. Susannah wiped it away instinctively. Fighting down waves of self-loathing for sleeping that long, she knelt by the bedside. "What's wrong? You feeling sad today? Did you think I'd gone out? I'm sorry. I just needed a quick rest. I wasn't trying to leave you all alone. Here, do you want me to switch the tape over for you? Are you ready for more *Odyssey*?"

Kitty stared at the wall, and Susannah turned to look, half expecting to find something there. "What is it?" she asked. "Does your tummy hurt?"

A pout. *No.*

"Are you wet? Do we need to get you changed?"

A scowl.

"Were you worried that I was gone for too long?"

No.

"What's wrong then?" She tried to follow her sister's eyes, which were now focused on the nightstand. Susannah picked up the picture of her mom at least ten years younger and twenty pounds lighter than she'd been when she died.

"Is that it?" she asked. "Do you miss Mom?"

Blink.

Susannah reached out and stroked Kitty's cheek. Her skin was clammy.

"I miss her too." Most days, Susannah would force cheer into her voice and say something like, *But at least we can thank Jesus that one day we'll all be together again*, or *I'm glad that we have each other.*

But today, all she had the energy to do was stroke her sister's tear-streaked face and repeat, "I miss her too."

CHAPTER 32

April 5

Darling, what a long day. Thank you so much for your prayers for me. Even though we didn't get a chance to talk much this week, I've felt your prayers lifting me up and encouraging me through all the plans and extra work. If it weren't for that, I'm not sure how I could have made it to tonight!

The ceremony was perfect. Mom was gorgeous, but of course no surprises there. I wish you could have seen Kitty. At first, we weren't sure if she'd feel up to it. You know how she can get kind of particular about things. Pouty. She's the sweetest, kindest soul in the world, but she can hold a grudge if she thinks you've ignored her too long! And Mom's been so busy, and last night Kitty wouldn't even talk to her, so we were all pretty worried.

But today she was on her best behavior. Mom let her wear that hot-pink bridesmaid dress, the one she wore the night of my prom. I'll have to send you some pictures soon. She was beautiful, and she knew it too. That girl can be so vain! But I think she realized she had to behave herself if she wanted everyone to be able to see her looking so pretty, and she did great. You should have heard it. Right when the pastor got to the part where he told Derek to kiss the bride, Kitty let out a huge snort. Derek and Mom were both laughing so hard, and so was everyone else, it hardly counted as a kiss when they finally got to it.

I wish you could have been there. I really do. But I think Mom was right. There was so much going on it wouldn't have really given us any time to spend together, and having you here at Mom's wedding would have gotten all the folks at church talking, and you can imagine what that's like in a small town like ours.

I just can't wait for when you do come visit, though. I can't believe we'll actually be spending Easter together. I'm sure other people could find a more romantic holiday, but I think it's a perfect symbol of how the blood of Christ brought us together. I can't wait.

Well, it's nearly eleven, and I'm completely exhausted, and I've got to get up early tomorrow. I know it's silly, but I'm actually nervous about taking care of Kitty this week. It's nothing I haven't done before. I just haven't done it this many days in a row by myself. But Mom and Derek deserve this honeymoon, and I'm not going to complain at all. Still, I'd love your prayers, ok? I can't believe what an encouragement you've become to me. I probably don't say it enough, so thank you.

Blessings,
Your Susannah

CHAPTER 33

Well, God, you brought me through another long morning. I don't know how you managed, but you did.

Susannah relished the sound of the hot water filling up the tub. She couldn't remember the last time she'd enjoyed a long bath. After checking one last time to make sure Kitty was still napping soundly, she put on one of her mom's old instrumental worship CDs and sank into the tub.

The Lord is my strength and my shield, an ever-present help in times of trouble.

She shut her eyes, letting the water fill all the way to the top.

The lions may grow weak and hungry, but those who seek the Lord lack no good thing.

She hummed along with the soft piano and violin music and thought about some of her favorite verses from Psalms.

Delight yourself in the Lord, and he will give you the desires of your heart.

God had given her so much. A close family. Almost two

decades with a kind, gentle mother who taught her about the Lord and modeled how to be a selfless servant to others.

A few months of excitement and happiness when she'd thought she'd found the man she wanted to marry.

Comfort even in the worst of troubles.

The Lord is good, and his love endures forever.

Maybe she didn't always feel the Holy Spirit like she had last Sunday at church, but she could never doubt his love. He'd blessed her life in so many ways, given her so many opportunities, surrounded her with so many people who loved her ...

If only he hadn't taken them each out of her life one by one until only she and Kitty remained.

Weeping may last for the night, but rejoicing comes in the morning.

That's what she had to focus on. God's love and mercy and goodness. There was no point dwelling on painful memories. She didn't want to grow old and bitter. She wanted God's love to pour out of her freely. Effortlessly. Abundantly.

Even if she never fell in love again.

Lord, why do I keep thinking about him? Why can't I get him out of my mind?

She hated to admit it, but ever since Grandma Lucy's

prayer at church, she'd been allowing thoughts of Scott to steal more and more of her mental energy. There had to be something else to focus on.

Christmas is in only ten days, Lord. Just ten more days ...

She still remembered the afternoon she'd come home from her shift at Winter Grove last fall and saw her mom mixing dough. "What are you making?"

"Friendship bread starter. If I get it ready now, we can make a batch to welcome Scott when he comes here to meet you."

Susannah had looked forward to that visit with the childish hopes of a five-year-old waiting for Santa's sleigh. Ten days until she finally saw Scott face to face, heard his voice for real instead of through electronic wires. Looked into his eyes.

Just ten more days ...

Susannah shut off the bath water and counted again to make sure she'd done the math right.

Ten days until Christmas.

She stood up, ignoring the cold chill that seeped through her skin.

Ten more days.

If she threw things together today, the starter would be ready to make Amish friendship bread Christmas morning.

Mom might be gone, sorrow might pour out of every one of her pores until she didn't know how she could even breathe, but Susannah was going to give her sister a joyful Christmas whether she felt like it or not.

CHAPTER 34

April 20

Dear Scott,

Happy Easter. Or maybe I should say happy Resurrection Day. I started out this morning really discouraged since I'd been looking forward to your visit so much, but I'm convinced God knows what he's doing. I wanted to give you an update on Kitty too. Her fever's a little elevated, but after Mom called Doctor Bell and talked to her on the phone, she said that we don't have to take her in yet. Just a lot of extra fluids. Mom's got a timer going. Every ten minutes one of us goes in and measures out 3 CCs of water. That's all. And we do our best to squirt it into the back of her mouth so it can go down by itself and she doesn't have to work too hard swallowing it.

We missed church today, so we had our own Easter worship service right there in Kitty's room. It was actually bittersweet. I have the greatest family in the world, Mom's found the man of her dreams (after Dad, of course), but I couldn't be perfectly happy because this was the weekend you and I were supposed to finally meet. I know that God must have good plans for this, but it's hard.

Instead of whining, though, I want to tell you about one of our favorite Easter traditions. Mom started it back when we were little girls, and I'm sure we'll be doing it still when she's eighty years old! So what we do is Mom gets those little plastic eggs from the store, but instead of hiding candy inside, she writes out either the name of a song or a Bible reference. It doesn't sound like much, but it's really elaborate. I think I counted last year and it's something like thirty eggs total. By the time you open them all and either read the passage or sing the hymn, you've gone through the entire Easter story from Palm Sunday to the Ascension. It's really neat.

One of the best parts (apart from the singing, which is my favorite), is hiding the eggs for Kitty. She's hilarious. We put them all over the house and then one of us (this year it was Derek, who Kitty just adores) pushes her in her wheelchair. When she spots one, she'll let us know, and that's how we do our Easter egg hunt. It's harder than it sounds, though, because it's over two dozen eggs and you have to hide them all at Kitty's eye level. So unless you want to put them all on a table, it takes a lot of creativity coming up with good spots.

Derek got us all really bad with one that he hid. You know where he put it? He had a blue egg, and he put it on the kitchen counter … inside our carton of farm-fresh eggs from Safe Anchorage (it's that goat farm I was telling you about with the neat gift shop where I got that stationary for those letters I've sent you). Anyway, at the farm they've got regular hens who lay regular brown eggs, but they've also got this special kind they call Easter eggers who lay blue eggs! So when Derek hid one in there, it took us all forever to find it. We finally had to give up. You should have heard Kitty laugh when she saw where he'd put it.

Speaking of Kitty, even though Dr. Bell didn't seem too worried, please keep her in your prayers. I know we'll talk tonight when you call, and I'm sure you'll remember to pray for her then (I love our prayer times together, by the way!), but Mom's really worried, and I know we could all use a little extra encouragement today from the Lord.

I hope it was a good day for you too. I miss you, which is kind of goofy to say, but it's true. I wish you were here. You would adore Kitty. She's so amazing. I can't wait until you get to meet her.

Yours,
Susannah

CHAPTER 35

"Come on, Kitty. Time to wake up."

Susannah tried to remember if her mom always ran into this much trouble rousing Kitty from her afternoon naps.

She touched her sister's forehead. She didn't feel hot, but she'd been acting more tired than usual, taking more time to wake up, sleeping longer each afternoon.

Maybe it was the winter.

Or was she depressed? Susannah didn't even know how to begin guessing if it was something like that. Should she call Dr. Bell? Would she be able to help or just refer her to a specialist in Spokane or Wenatchee?

She rolled her sister onto her back and checked her diaper. It wasn't wet, which was convenient for the moment, but Susannah knew from experience that if Kitty's bladder didn't kick in soon, by the time her systems finally caught up with each other she'd leak right through the Depends and all over the mattress.

Well, that's what the chux pads on the bed were for. Not worth worrying over.

"Wake up, Kitty. It's time for your snack. And after you eat, you can help me make a Christmas treat. Would you like that?"

Kitty lifted up a single finger.

"Oh, come on," Susannah prodded. "I thought you'd be way more excited than that."

Kitty made a fist with her hand.

"That's more like it. If your back's not too tight, I think we'll save your massage until later and I'll get you into your chair."

Blink.

After helping Kitty manage to drink five ounces of formula without gagging, Susannah pulled ingredients down from the cupboards and chatted with her sister, who watched from her wheelchair.

"All right, so we'll need flour and sugar, and I'm pretty sure we still have yeast in the fridge, but I better proof it to make sure it's good."

When she was alive, Susannah's mom made homemade bread once or twice a week on top of the cinnamon rolls and other pastries for Sunday school or Bible studies. Susannah should have been a baking expert by now for all the times she'd helped in the kitchen, but she'd never progressed past the very basics.

Oh, well. At least she knew how to follow directions.

She pulled down her mom's index cards from the cupboard and ran her finger along the little hand-painted flowers. Susannah had made her the recipe holder as a Mother's Day gift several years earlier. As far as she could remember, it was the last time she'd picked up a paintbrush.

After pulling out the rest of the ingredients, Susannah set to work, being careful to keep up her one-sided conversation with her sister. She wanted Kitty to feel engaged, and she also wanted to keep her from falling asleep in her chair. Why couldn't she remember if it was normal for Kitty to be so drowsy in the afternoons? Why hadn't she paid better attention, asked more questions when her mom was alive?

For the first few minutes, she was afraid she'd have to throw out the yeast, wait for Derek to buy her some more, and start the whole batch over in a few days when it would be too late for Christmas morning, but thankfully the bubbles finally started to form, filling the kitchen with a familiar yeasty smell.

The smell of love. The smell of a peaceful family life. The smell of Mom.

Kitty grunted with pleasure.

"I know," Susannah told her, "it's going to be delicious."

She didn't stop to think how wasteful it was to make a whole batch of Amish friendship bread for Christmas breakfast when she was the only one who would be able to enjoy any. It was the entire experience. Susannah couldn't remember a single Christmas when she didn't wake up to the smell of Mom's baking. Kitty might not be able to eat anything Susannah prepared, but at least it would remind her — remind them both really — of happier times.

Times when Mom was alive, when the future was bright and promising, when Susannah could joyfully ease through her day without those relentless reminders that all her hopes and dreams and plans had come crashing down around her.

CHAPTER 36

June 3

Dear Scott,

I can't believe it's summer. Well, I can because Orchard Grove gets *hot* this time of year, but what I mean is I can't believe you're meeting up with the Kingdom Builders interns today and I won't be there.

Do you sometimes feel like God has it out for us? I mean, I'm mostly joking, but do you ever wonder? I've prayed about our relationship a lot. Probably more than I've prayed about anything other than getting to the mission field. And each time I pray, I do my best to surrender and tell God that I want his will more than my own. That if you and I aren't meant to be together, I'd rather find that out sooner than later.

But each time I ask God if we're where we're supposed to be, I feel so strongly that we are. I look back at how we met, at how our very first conversation wasn't about going to the movies or what restaurant to eat at but about missions. And it just seems so clear to me that God brought us together for a reason. I'm doing my best to still stay guarded, but I can't stop thinking about a future together with you. I can't stop thinking about what it would be like to serve God around the world next to someone so godly and strong, who knows my emotions, who is so kind to me.

You are the first man I've ever felt this way about, and that's partly what makes today so hard. I feel like when you hop on that plane with the interns, I'm losing you. It's probably silly. It's probably me just being girly and babyish about it all, but that's what this feels like. I keep telling God that I was supposed to come with you all on that trip.

But Kitty's not getting any better. Dr. Bell stopped by last night. It was really sweet of her. She knows Kitty gets anxious about going anywhere and that the stress can really complicate her digestive issues, so she came by instead of making us drive out to her office. She doesn't think we need to go to the hospital yet, but if Kitty can't start eating again in a day or two, she'll need some IVs at the very least. Dr. Bell was thinking about antibiotics because her lungs sound a little more gunky than normal, which could be the start of pneumonia, but Mom wants to hold off and stick to some of the homeopathics for now. I understand where she's coming from. You give Kitty one dose of antibiotics, and she'll still be letting you know about it a month later (or at least her gut will).

Anyway, I'll spare you the details, and I'm sorry if this email started off a little depressing. I'm doing all right. Just miss you. I'll be praying for you and the interns. I've got the clock in my room set to Korea time so I'll be able to keep better track of what you're doing. Please be safe and come back soon. We'll have so much catching up to do, and I know my nights are going to be terribly quiet and lonely until you're home.

Please know that while you go out and serve the Lord, I'll be praying for you hourly (probably more!) and holding you very close to my heart.

Yours always,
Susannah

CHAPTER 37

Susannah was gathering the supplies she needed for Kitty's sponge bath when the doorbell rang. Who would be stopping by here in the middle of the day?

She made sure her sister was comfortably propped up with her pillows and then trudged to the front door. She had no idea why she was moving so slowly. Usually, the holidays made her feel renewed and energized, but this year she only felt exhausted.

She peered into the peephole, surprised to see who it was. She opened the door.

"Hi." She knew she must be desperate for company if the sight of Ricky Fields could bring such a rush of warm relief. "Would you like to step in?"

He cleared his throat and kept his eyes on Susannah's feet. "I can't stay long." He held out a colorful tray of Christmas cookies like a protective shield. "My mom made these for you. Said I should drop them off. Said she remembered how much your mom liked baking and worried that maybe you and your sister didn't have anything nice for Christmas."

In all the time she'd known Ricky Fields, she wasn't sure she'd ever heard so many words come out of his mouth at once. He looked both exhausted and flushed from the effort.

"That's really sweet." She took the tray, which he seemed somewhat reluctant to hand over. "Why don't you come in and say hi to Kitty?"

He cleared his throat again. Susannah wanted to cough on his behalf. "I can, but only for a minute. Mom's in the car waiting." He offered a sheepish grin.

"That's fine," Susannah said. "She's been pretty tired this week anyway."

"Yeah," Ricky answered, "I know what you mean."

Susannah had no idea what he was talking about, but she waved quickly to Mrs. Fields, who was parked in the driveway, and stepped aside to let Ricky through. She glanced around the living room, thankful to find it free from random socks or bras or other embarrassing clutter.

After asking Ricky to wash his hands to keep from spreading any germs, she led him down the hall. Thinking about how excited her sister would be, she stopped outside Kitty's door and whispered, "You wait here. I want it to be a surprise."

Ricky grinned conspiratorially.

Susannah hurried into her sister's room and covered Kitty's lap and legs with a heavy quilt, the result of an overzealous sense of modesty inherited from her mother. "There's someone here to see you," she told her sister. "Want to guess who it is?"

Kitty grunted and slapped her thigh. Her eyes widened gleefully, and for a second, Susannah was paralyzed with fear. What if Kitty thought it was their mom? How could Susannah explain away that kind of disappointment?

She forced a smile on her face. "Here's a hint. He looks very, very handsome."

Susannah had forgotten that Ricky was right outside the door and could hear every word she said. Her remark was met with a hiccup from the hall and a loud snort from the bed.

Kitty slapped her thigh once more.

Susannah put on a melodramatic frown. "Then again, you've been pretty tired. I guess I should tell him you're napping. A girl needs her beauty sleep, right?"

Two slaps.

Susannah shrugged. "All right. I guess I can let him in for a minute, but you better behave yourself or you'll be in big trouble, got that?" Even while she tried to sound firm, she couldn't keep the grin off her face. She reached into the hallway and beckoned a somewhat sheepish-looking Ricky inside.

Kitty tensed up every working muscle in her body.

"I think she's happy to see you." Susannah smiled.

Ricky stepped up to the bedside, no longer hiccupping. "Hi, Kitty. How's it going?"

Susannah was about to answer for her out of habit but then stepped back against the wall and waited.

"That's a pretty nightgown," Ricky told her. "Is it one of the ones your mom made for you?"

Kitty lifted one leg, and Susannah automatically translated, "Yes."

"I like it." Ricky paused for a minute, and as she stared at his back Susannah realized his shoulders had broadened out quite a bit since the night of the homeschool prom. Ricky shoved his hands into his pockets. "Well, I gave your sister some Christmas cookies. My mom made them special for you two. She wanted you to have them. I've got to go now, but if it's all right with you and your sister, maybe I'll come say hi again. Would that be ok?"

A kick, two blinks, and a smile so big there was no need for an interpretation.

Ricky finished saying goodbye, and Susannah followed him down the hall. "That was really sweet of you. Let me grab my boots and I'll say thanks to your mom."

"You don't have to do that," Ricky insisted. "I mean, the

walkway's really icy. I wouldn't want you to slip."

Susannah hadn't left the house since she'd gone to church last Sunday. She'd had no reason to worry about the condition of her walkway.

"You got any salt?" Ricky asked. "Or maybe some gravel? I could stand it down for you real quick before I leave."

"Don't worry. I'll take care of it later."

"You sure? It's no problem if you just tell me where everything is."

"No," Susannah insisted, embarrassed to admit she had no idea where to start looking for anything like that. "I need an excuse to get some fresh air anyway. Tell your mom thanks, and I'm glad you came in to say hi to Kitty. She'll be talking about your visit for weeks."

Ricky gave her a quizzical glance and then a shrug. "All right. Have a good night."

"Yeah, you too." Susannah realized she didn't want him to leave. She was about to tell him there might be some ice melt in the garage, but he was already out the door and down the walkway.

"Merry Christmas," she called out after him, but her words died in the cold air, and he didn't turn around.

CHAPTER 38

June 21

Dear Scott,

I had a really good talk with Mom today! She and Derek had just gotten home from a breakfast date, and she looked dazzling. She wasn't dressed fancy or anything, and her only jewelry is her wedding ring, but she was stunning. I think— no, I know — that the beauty comes from being loved by her new husband so much.

I'm so glad they found each other. I didn't think Mom would ever get remarried, and maybe it would have been harder when I was younger. I can see myself getting jealous or feeling threatened, but Derek's a kind and godly man, and he has a great sense of humor. He's perfect for Mom. She's laughed more in the last few months than I think she has in the past fifteen years!

And that's a really cute story too. Did I ever tell it to you? He moved to Orchard Grove a couple years ago, but he goes to the different church on the other side of town, mostly because he's a welder and wakes up crazy early during the week, so Sundays he likes to sleep in and go to the afternoon service at Valley Tabernacle. Last summer, the two churches did a joint VBS program, which makes it a little hard to organize since both congregations are involved. So Derek signed up to help with recreation, and Mom always does snacks for everyone, and for some reason they were both expecting to use the same part of the fellowship hall downstairs, him for games and her for feeding the kids. I guess the first day they met they nearly got into a fight over it until he apologized and then was extra nice trying to make it up to her. It hasn't even been quite a year since their first date, but they're perfect for each other.

I'm so glad my mom's found someone that makes her happy. And I'm glad she's comfortable with the two of us talking as much as we do. Sometimes she worries that I'm not getting enough sleep, but she says she's thankful for the times you've called her just so she feels like you're not a stranger. Speaking of phone calls, I miss talking to you! I know you're really busy over there, and I pray for you and the interns every time I think of you (which is quite a bit). I hope those Bible verses I copied down are encouraging to you when you feel tired or homesick.

Don't forget that you have a friend out here in Orchard Grove praying for your safe return.

Love,
Susannah

CHAPTER 39

Kitty had been so excited about her visit from Ricky (aka Prince Charming) that it was after 9:30 by the time she finally fell asleep.

Susannah was behind on just about everything — the laundry, the dishes, the grocery list she was supposed to pass on to Derek.

She staggered her way into the kitchen, groaning inwardly at the sight of all the dirty plates and bowls. When was the last time she'd cleaned up after herself?

She still didn't understand how her mom had managed to cook three nutritious meals a day plus keep up on all of Kitty's care and the other chores around the house. Just making herself a simple pot of soup could throw off Susannah's schedule for a week.

Well, Lord, I never claimed to be perfect. I guess this is just one area where you'll have to keep on teaching me how to improve and until then, help me show myself some grace.

She stared at the huge platter of cookies Ricky had

dropped off and wondered if his mom realized Kitty couldn't handle any foods besides her formula. Oh, well. It looked festive, and she could share some with Derek tomorrow when he dropped off the next batch of groceries.

She took out a pecan shortbread cookie and nibbled around the buttery edges. Once she got the dishes clean, she'd treat herself to another. Her enthusiasm lasted about two seconds. It could take hours just to catch up on the kitchen, and she'd still be behind on every other part of the house.

God, I'm sorry I didn't help Mom out more when she was alive. I'm sorry I took her for granted for so long.

She left the light on over the sink — an optimistic symbol of her plans to return to cleaning — and made her way to her computer. She'd been so busy she hadn't checked her email in a week or more.

Not that she expected to hear from anybody in particular.

She waited for the desktop to start up. It was an old hand-me-down from Derek and took ten minutes just to load. Still, it was better than nothing. Her mom had been fairly suspicious of the internet, so Susannah had never gotten involved in social media or online shopping or anything like that. Right now, all she wanted was a reason to procrastinate. An excuse to forget about the dirty kitchen, the endless pile of dishes, those countless other chores she hadn't done today and might not get to tomorrow either.

When her inbox finally loaded, it told her what she already knew. No messages.

It was her own fault. She'd been clear in her last email to Scott that she didn't think they should communicate any more.

At all.

Still, sometimes she wondered how she'd react to finding a note from him. Something like *hi, how are you doing, merry Christmas, do you still want to marry me?*

She shook her head. Her mom had spent sixteen years as a single parent before she met Derek, and she never complained. Never pined away for some stranger on the other side of the country.

God, I know I worry as much as my mother, but I wish you would have let me inherit some of her positive qualities too, like her patience.

The nights were the hardest, with Kitty already asleep and Susannah too restless to go to bed but too exhausted to tackle the chores that kept piling higher and higher. Cold winter nights, seemingly endless.

She could email him. It wouldn't take more than two or three minutes. *Hi Scott, it's me. Just wanted to wish you a merry Christmas. I hope you're doing well.*

What could it hurt?

She opened up a new message but stopped herself before her fingers even found their place on the keyboard. No. Resuming their relationship, no matter how casual it started out, would only make it that much harder for them both to move on. And that's what Susannah needed to do. Move on.

Instead of writing him, she sent a quick email to Ricky and his mom thanking them both for the Christmas cookies. Nobody else from church had thought to do anything like that. The way some people treated her now, it was as if her mom had never existed. Never served on the hospitality committee at Orchard Grove for decades, never organized all those meal trains for new mothers or church members recovering from surgeries.

Maybe it was easier for the women of Orchard Grove to ignore the past, but Susannah never could. Her mom had done so much for others, and now she was purged from memory when she'd only been dead four months.

I'm sorry for grumbling, Lord. Please forgive me.

After expressing her gratitude to the Fields, she made her way back to the kitchen. She'd given up trying to convince herself to get anything clean before tomorrow. Now she just had to turn off the lights, lock herself in, and call it a night. As she reached for the light switch behind the sink, a Ziploc bag behind the microwave caught her attention.

She sighed. All that work and she'd completely forgotten about the starter mix she'd made earlier in the week. Cringing slightly at what she knew was coming, she opened the bag. She didn't even have to get her nose close to know it was rancid. Using significantly more force than necessary, she heaved it in the direction of the trash can and missed. Moldy starter landed on the floor, the cupboard, and the fridge.

She sank to her knees, too tired to even grab a rag. She used the old Ziploc to smear up as much as she could and made her way to bed. She'd clean up the rest tomorrow.

By the time she reached her room, tears of loneliness and frustration and hot, inexplicable anger poured down her cheeks and splashed onto the cluttered floor beneath her.

CHAPTER 40

July 9

Dear Scott,

I'm so glad you're back home! I know we're still thousands of miles apart, but it's still so comforting to know that you have internet access now and that I can email you any time I want without having to wonder how long it will take for you to read it. And actually hearing your voice again! I still can't believe how late we stayed up last night, but there was so much catching up to do!

I loved your story about the missionary in Mongolia who had to butcher a sheep in his bathtub. It was hilarious. I told Mom and Derek. She though it was gross, but he laughed his head off. Then he talked about how when he was a young man, he'd thought about doing mission work too. It was neat because I didn't know that about him before. Mom said she could see the two of them doing short-term trips at some point, and it just got me thinking. God can use people at any age. I've been so impatient to get to the mission field now, but I have a whole lifetime ahead of me! So what if I have to wait another few years? If God has plans for me to spend my life overseas serving him, it's going to happen no matter how long it takes me to get there!

That's helping me be patient about finding the right time for you to visit, too. Mom says the beginning part of August will work out well over here. We can talk about that next time you call. In the meantime, I know God's using everything — our relationship, Kitty's health, even Mom and Derek's marriage — to teach me to wait on him and on his perfect timing.

Thank you for being patient with me. I appreciate you more than I know how to put into words.

Always yours,
Susannah

CHAPTER 41

Susannah was halfway through Kitty's dinner when the doorbell rang.

"That's Derek with the groceries," Susannah told her sister. "I'll be right back."

Blink.

She smoothed out her hair as she made her way down the hall and opened the door. "Hey."

"Howdy, howdy."

She tried to match her stepdad's playful grin but got the feeling she failed pathetically.

"How you doing today? You ready for an early Christmas present?" Derek stepped past her and set the bags of groceries on the dining room table where Kitty was sitting in her chair. "Hi, pretty lady." He tousled the top of Kitty's head. "What's for dinner tonight? Delectable vanilla or scrumptious strawberry?"

Kitty let out am amused snort.

"Thanks for the groceries," Susannah told him. "What do

I owe you?"

Derek ignored the question and picked up Kitty's bottle of formula. "This all you've eaten for dinner so far?" he asked her playfully. "Come on. I know you can do better than that."

"We got a later start than normal," Susannah tried to explain, but he cut her off.

"Enough of that now. You bundle up and grab your boots. It's a little icy, but not too bad. Remind me before I go and I'll salt the walkway for you." He lowered himself into the chair where Susannah usually fed her sister.

"Are you staying for dinner?" she asked, wondering what she could possibly offer him. She'd finished off the last of the bean soup at lunchtime and hadn't thought about what to make next. She'd probably grab a bowl of cereal for dinner and make herself a pot of something more nutritious tomorrow.

Or the next day.

"I'm staying," he answered, "but you're going."

"What?"

Derek kept his back to her and opened the bottle of formula. "This is it. Your early Christmas present. Oh, I almost forgot." He reached into his pocket and pulled out some crisp twenty-dollar bills. "Go out. Take yourself shopping. Get one of those mandy-paddies or whatever you girls call those things. I don't care. Just come back here with a story of how you spoiled yourself, all right? Tonight's all on me."

Susannah stared at the money he'd shoved into her hand. "You really didn't have to …"

Derek's smile was ill-suited for the brusque tone he was trying to adopt. "I don't want to hear another word out of you until you've come back and are ready to share all the ways you wasted my money on yourself, got that? And I better not catch you home before —" he gave his watch an exaggerated frown "— nine o'clock. Nine o'clock with none of the money left and at least two or three good stories of how you pampered yourself."

"But I really have to …"

"Get on, go." He nudged her playfully. "Before I change my mind and give you even more cash."

Susannah glanced back once at Kitty, who was thrilled to see her sister bested. Susannah couldn't help but smile back. "All right. I'll be …"

"Yeah, yeah." Derek waved his hands in the air. "You'll be back later, goodnight, thanks so much, all that good stuff. Now get out of here, kiddo, before I tell Ricky Fields you're free for a night on the town."

The jocularity was too much for Kitty, who started to laugh and sprayed formula onto Derek's shirt.

Susannah paused for a minute, wondering if he remembered where the rags were, but he wiped himself down with a corner of the tablecloth, turned to her, and said this time in a normal voice, "Go have a little fun, all right? Do some Christmas shopping, stretch your legs. It will do you good."

Susannah nodded. "Ok, thanks."

"Drive carefully," he told her, and in their eyes passed the echoes of sadness they both shared.

"I will."

"Watch out for the ice on the walkway!" he called after her, and then Susannah was outside and alone, with a hundred dollars in cash and no idea what she was going to do with herself for the next three hours.

CHAPTER 42

July 25

Dear Scott,

Nine more days! Can you believe it? Then we'll be together. I hope you like carbs because Mom's planning to bake up a storm. It's a good thing you're not on a diet or anything since she's a fabulous cook. I wish I could be more like her!

I know it's selfish, but I'm so glad you're home. I'm sure you were a real blessing to the interns. You know, for a while I was disappointed I couldn't go, but I see now how it will be even more special when the first time we meet face to face it will be with my whole family here. They're all going to love you. I just know it.

Something you need to know about Derek is he's always joking, so don't let him get under your skin. Whatever he says, it's teasing. It's taken me time to get used to because for so long our family was really serious, but now it's joking,

174

joking, joking all the time. Just yesterday, Derek took that photograph Kitty loves so much where she's in the prom dress, and he cut out Jim Carey's face from *The Mask* and taped it over the face of the boy she's dancing with. He just did it during the night while she was sleeping, and then this morning we all woke up to her laughing so hard she almost choked. It took fifteen minutes just to get her calm enough that she could breathe normally again! But it wasn't anything to worry about. It was just fun. She's not due for her checkup for a few more days, but she's doing so much better. It never did turn into pneumonia either, thank God. But I'm still glad I stayed home from the summer trip because otherwise I would have been spending so much time worrying about her.

Nine days! I sometimes think this must be some sort of dream. We've tried so many times to get together and it never worked. Now I think God was saving it so the first meeting would be extra special, just like I know it will be.

Mom asked me if I was nervous to meet you, but I'm not. Just excited. Excited to finally know what it's like to have you right there while we're talking. It's going to be wonderful. See you soon. (I can't believe I just wrote that!)

Yours,
Susannah

CHAPTER 43

Susannah hadn't had a night off since her mom died. It took her five minutes sitting in the driveway before she convinced herself to put the car into reverse instead of running back into the house and telling Derek she would take care of Kitty's dinner.

Getting out of her own driveway was the first obstacle. Deciding where to go was the next. It wasn't like Orchard Grove had big malls or shopping centers. The Christian bookstore had gone out of business last year, and the only real friends her age had left Orchard Grove after graduating.

She passed the road to Ricky Field's home, and for a brief second she thought about stopping by. But what would she say? What would be the point? She drove on and realized she was hungry. She had money but refused to walk into a diner and eat a meal alone, which is how she soon found herself at the Walmart food court.

She sat down with a grilled chicken salad, wishing she

brought a book with her or something else to do to pass the time. Her Bible maybe.

God, I'm thankful that Derek is giving me this night off. I just wish I had known about it beforehand so I could be prepared.

She thought about the cash in her purse, about what kind of Christmas present she should find for Kitty. Then something for herself too. Derek had been adamant about that.

Good thing she was at Walmart, where she could find everything she would ever need or want, throw it in a shopping cart, and make it home in time to put Kitty to bed at eight. It wasn't until she started eating her salad that she realized how much her body was craving fresh produce. Her mom had always kept the fridge stocked with healthy foods, creating elaborate meal plans far more varied and wholesome than bowl after bowl of leftover soup. Susannah knew the basics of cooking. She just didn't have the energy to justify making big fancy dinners when she was the only one who could eat them.

Christmas would be her first meal that didn't come out of a single pot in months. Derek would come over in the afternoon with a ham, and she was supposed to think up a few sides. Nothing fancy, since it would only be her and her sister and her stepdad. Maybe she'd find a pre-made crust and make an apple pie for dessert.

Speaking of desserts, she should probably use this night off to drive down to Baxter Loop and buy some of the Amish Friendship bread starter there instead of wandering the aisles at Walmart, praying for inspiration. Safe Anchorage Farms had the best gift shop in at least fifty miles. She could head over there, get a new batch of starter, pick presents for both Derek and Kitty, and find some stationary for herself too.

It beat pushing a shopping cart around a crowded supermarket.

As soon as she finished her salad, she braced for the cold and headed back toward her car, trying to remember the quickest way from here to Baxter Loop.

Maybe Derek really had known what he was doing with this surprise night off.

Maybe it would be a good evening after all.

CHAPTER 44

August 3

I don't even know what to say. I feel like after all your encouragement last night and the way you prayed for me and the love of Christ you showed me, I should have something really significant or profound to tell you, but I don't.

Mom is gone. I still can't get that into my head. I'm never going to hear her playing the piano again, leading our family in hymns. Never going to wake up to the smell of her bread rising.

I shouldn't feel so numb. I should be sobbing my heart out, but I haven't even cried since last night when you prayed for me.

Mom was my rock. Maybe that sounds blasphemous to say since we're supposed to find our grounding in Christ, but now that she's gone I realize it was her.

Kitty's in bed. She's supposed to be up for her lunch by now, but I don't have the energy. She knows something's wrong. I've tried to tell her, but she doesn't understand what I'm talking about. She'll go on expecting Mom to come home every single day. I can't stand the thought of her suffering like that.

Can't stand the thought of life without Mom.

She's the one who prayed with me every morning and every night about my relationship with you, asking God to close doors and open doors and guide us in his will. Who will be praying for us now?

I'm sorry this is such a downer. I'm trying so hard to stay positive for Kitty, and I guess I just needed someone to vent to. Thank you for being my shoulder to cry on (metaphorically at least). I want to be with you. Just thought I'd write and let you know that.

Love,
Susannah

CHAPTER 45

It was a few minutes after seven as Susannah pulled up the long driveway of Safe Anchorage Farms. Hopefully the gift shop was still open.

She parked the car and hopped out, grateful to see the lights of the store still on. Bells jingled their welcome as she entered. A dozen scents, each one a slight variation of the next, wafted toward her. She ran her eyes over the labels of the soaps and candles made from Safe Anchorage goat milk. If Kitty didn't have such sensitive skin, she'd buy her one of the perfumed lotions. Maybe a nice candle instead. Susannah picked up the cinnamon and then the lilac, trying to decide which Kitty would prefer.

Connie, Grandma Lucy's niece who ran the shop, bustled out of a back room, wiping her hands on her apron. Her face lit up in a smile as her eyes landed on Susannah.

"Well, look who it is. Doing a little last-minute Christmas shopping?"

Susannah nodded.

"You see those journals in the back? We just got some new designs in last week."

"Oh, thanks. I just finished my old one."

Connie smiled. "Girl like you, it doesn't surprise me."

Susannah made a mental note to check them out before she left.

"Take your time looking around. Grandma Lucy stopped by for a visit, and we're going to be drinking tea here in the back, so just let me know when you're ready to check out. Better yet, if you're not in a rush, come and join us for a spell. It's nice to see you out and about. Who's watching your sister tonight?"

Susannah wondered what it might be like to live in a big city where the people she encountered had no idea about her past or her family situation. It couldn't feel lonelier than Orchard Grove, could it?

Susannah shivered from the cold. "A cup of tea sounds nice if you're sure I'm not intruding."

Connie shook her head. "You know Grandma Lucy. Nothing she loves more than a good visit."

Susannah followed her into the back room, where Grandma Lucy sat in a rocker that nearly swallowed her small frame. She reached out her warm hands to grasp Susannah's. "You're so cold. You aren't coming down with a virus, are you?"

Susannah shook her head. With as scared as her mom had been about Kitty catching a cold or flu, Susannah had been schooled from the earliest age in every single home remedy, herbal concoction, and over-the-counter homeopathic even suspected to boost immunity. It had been three or four years since her last sore throat.

"You just sit down here and visit," Connie said. "I just remembered I have bread rising I've got to check on. I'll only be a few minutes."

The mention of bread reminded Susannah why she'd stopped here in the first place. "Oh, do you have any friendship starter?"

"Sure do." Connie draped her knitted sweater over her apron and fastened the oversized buttons. "I'll bring you back some from the house. Help yourself to some tea. We've got plenty."

It wasn't until Connie left that Susannah realized how intensely Grandma Lucy was staring at her. Trying not to show her unease, Susannah reached out for the teapot. Her hands shook when she poured her drink "I was really encouraged by your prayer on Sunday," she offered weakly.

Grandma Lucy smiled. "Tell me how God spoke to you."

Susannah warmed her hands up on the teacup. "Well, I guess the part that stood out to me the most was about how

God finishes the work he starts in us. You quoted that verse in Isaiah about how he doesn't bring to the point of birth and then fail to carry out the delivery. I've been thinking about my own life, how it all fits together in his plans." Susannah was rambling. Her cheeks heated up.

"You're talking about the mission field?"

Susannah tried to hide the way her teacup trembled in her hand. "Yeah. Did my mom tell you about that or something?"

Grandma Lucy smiled. "No, dear. But you have *missionary* written all over your face. When you get to be my age, you see these things."

Susannah doubted that but didn't waste time arguing.

"So God has called you to the mission field." There wasn't a hint of a question in Grandma Lucy's statement.

"Well, I thought he had. But then there was the car accident, and now Kitty …" Susannah stopped short. When had she lost the basic mechanics of expressing herself? Had it really been that long since she'd sat down and visited with someone?

"You think God's forgotten you. You think he called you to the mission field and then changed his mind and abandoned you."

Susannah had never expressed her feelings in those terms

before, but she realized Grandma Lucy was right. "Yeah. It seems like it. I mean, I know …"

Grandma Lucy held up her hand for silence. Susannah waited patiently for an uncomfortable minute before Grandma Lucy spoke again, except this time she wasn't addressing Susannah.

"Lord, you know this young woman's dilemma. You know how earnestly her heart has longed for the mission field, but for this season you've called her to bloom where she's planted, and that makes her feel like you've deserted her entirely."

Susannah blushed to hear such a candid assessment of her spiritual state.

"Lord, we know that you are not a God of chaos. This confusion doesn't come from you, and so we rebuke it in the name of Jesus, and we ask that in its place you bring deep clarity. Show your child the secret of being content in any and every situation. Reaffirm your love for her. She spends many weary days filling others up and tending to their needs, and now we're asking you to do the same for her. Meet her where she is. Give her joy where she is. You're using this time to prepare her, sharpen her."

Something in Grandma Lucy's tone had changed. Even though she was still praying to God, Susannah got the distinct impression that she was speaking to her. Preaching to her. Pouring encouragement into her battle-weary soul.

"Show her that not a day of her calling will be lost. You still have plans for her that extend beyond Orchard Grove, beyond Washington State, to the very ends of the earth. You will go with her, guiding her each step through fire and rain and storm, and in each chapter of her life you will be there, leading and protecting her. You are her good shepherd. You have laid down your life for her, just as she wants to lay down her life for you. You've seen the sacrifices she's made, and in your good plans you will restore all that was once lost."

Restore. There was that word again. Susannah didn't want to believe. Didn't want to set herself up for even more disappointment, but hope was calling to her. Beckoning to her. She couldn't resist.

Yes, Lord. I will hope in you, and I will find the courage to trust you to restore everything I gave up. Just give me the patience to wait until that day.

Grandma Lucy was silent, and Susannah looked up at her to see if her eyes were open. Grandma Lucy was staring at her with a look that was so frank, so candid Susannah was certain the old woman had opened up her rib cage and was staring into her very soul.

The thought hit her like a burst of heat from the wood stove in the back of the room. *She knows about Scott.*

It was ridiculous. Her mom recognized how gossip could spread in a community like Orchard Grove. Neither she nor Susannah had mentioned Scott's visit to anyone but Derek, and he wasn't the type to go blabbing that sort of news around town.

Nobody had told Grandma Lucy about Scott, but she knew. Susannah was sure of it.

Grandma Lucy's eyes twinkled. There was a playfulness there, like when she and Derek joked with Kitty about her Prince Charming.

Maybe I should ask her.

The thought was as fleeting as it was absurd. What was she supposed to say? *Oh, by the way, Grandma Lucy, there's this guy I fell in love with almost a year ago. I've never met him, but there were times I was convinced we were going to get married. Except all that fell apart, so I'm wondering if you can tell me what plans God has for the two of us since you're so much better at hearing from him than I am.*

It was ridiculous. She shouldn't.

Couldn't.

Susannah opened her mouth.

"Here I am." The store bells jingled. "You're one lucky

girl. This is our last batch of starter until next week, and it's all yours." Connie bustled back into the room, shattering the spiritual intensity that hung heavy in the room after Grandma Lucy's prayer.

Connie sat down with a loud sigh. "I remember your mom making that friendship bread for Sunday school. She was such a good baker."

Susannah glanced at Grandma Lucy, who looked so serene. Like a sage.

I could still ask her, Susannah thought to herself. *Grandma Lucy knows something about my future.*

It was a silly assumption. If God wanted to tell Susannah about Scott, he could speak to her himself. There was no need to ask this old woman in her rocking chair. Besides, what gave Susannah the impression that Grandma Lucy could hear from God better than she could? Didn't all believers have access to the same Holy Spirit?

"It was a nice sermon Sunday, wasn't it?" Connie prattled.

Susannah made the appropriate replies to keep the conversation going, but she stole glances every now and then at Grandma Lucy, who appeared to be dozing off in her rocker.

Or maybe she was praying.

Praying for Susannah?

Praying for Susannah and Scott?

Susannah sat in the back for a few more minutes, then did a little bit of shopping until she'd found presents for Kitty and Derek as well as some stationary and a new journal for herself.

An hour after she arrived, she headed back into the dark night, started up the car, and began the winding drive home.

CHAPTER 46

August 12

Dear Scott,

I know you've been waiting for my response, and I'm sorry it's taken me these few days to get back to you. Please believe me when I tell you that they have been days full of prayers and tears, not just for my mom but also for what I'm about to tell you.

After everything that's happened here, I really don't see how anything could ever develop between us. Months ago you asked me to pray and ask God if he intended for this relationship to deepen. At first, I thought his answer was yes, but it's become more and more clear over the past few days that it was only wishful thinking on my part.

I know this email is going to be painful for you to read, and I'm sure I can trust you to understand how devastating it is for me to write. But Kitty needs me. I could never dream of deserting her, not that I'd ever picture you asking me to.

190

But that's the problem. Even when we talked on the phone, you made it clear that you were willing to give up your work for the Lord in order to be here with me. I know some girls might find it romantic for you to be so selfless, but the more I've thought about it and prayed about it, I can't ask you to make that kind of sacrifice for me.

From the very beginning of our relationship, I've prayed that neither of us would ever make the other one an idol. And if I allowed you to stop your missionary work or even put it on hold just so I could have you near me, I could never forgive myself. God has put such an incredible calling on your life. I know he has plans to continue using you to bring his glory to the nations, and I won't stand in your way.

One of the hardest things God has ever asked me to do is surrender our relationship to him, especially after losing my mom. She was so excited to meet you, and I'm probably never going to understand why God took her home when he did. But I simply have to trust that his timing is perfect, and that means that it's time for me to give up my dreams for the mission field and release you with a full and tender heart.

I'm so sorry. None of this is your fault, and I'm afraid now that you'll just think I was stringing you along for all those months. You were so patient with me, so gracious. You didn't want to move fast because you know I'm young and you knew my mom wanted to meet you in person before she could give her official blessing to our relationship. But now that can never happen, and as much as I selfishly want to keep talking to you every night, emailing you about my day, I've come to realize it's best for us to say goodbye now instead of dragging out a painful parting.

I know we'll both mourn as we think about the things that could have been, and I want you to know that I will always pray for your happiness and blessings. Please believe me when I tell you that God has amazing plans for you, plans to continue spreading his gospel to the farthest corners of the earth. Unfortunately, I see now that if I were to hold onto this friendship that has grown to mean so much to me, I would be standing in your way and the calling God has placed upon your spirit.

You are a kind, godly man, and I consider myself so honored that you invested so much into my life. I will hold these months tenderly in my memories and remember you in my prayers for as long as I live.

Blessings,
Susannah

CHAPTER 47

Kitty was fussy and inconsolable. Once Susannah got home, it took close to an hour to calm her down.

"I'm sorry," Derek apologized before he left. "I wanted to give you a night off, but I guess too much time has passed. She's not used to me anymore."

"She just misses Mom." Susannah knew the words had been a mistake when she saw the pain tear through Derek's eyes. She reached out her hand to touch him on the elbow. There was something comforting about that quick exchange. "It's late," she added before she got too emotional. "Thanks again. It was really thoughtful of you."

Derek offered a small smile. "Well, I hope it was relaxing for you. I get concerned about you here all by yourself. You know that, don't you?"

She forced a smile. "Don't worry. We've got everything we need. And thanks again for coming by with the groceries. It's such a huge blessing."

"Well, I wish sometimes you'd ask me to bring by more

193

than cereal and dried beans."

"I will. We're still figuring all this out."

He nodded. "Yes, we are."

She wished him goodnight, spent a few minutes tidying up the house, and took her bag from Safe Anchorage to her room. She pulled the gift items out one by one and set them behind some boxes on a closet shelf to stay hidden until Christmas. She'd found Derek a traveler's coffee mug with blue forget-me-nots she was certain would remind him of her mom. For Kitty, she bought a framed copy of the Beatitudes to hang on her wall and new yarn to make a nice lap blanket. Susannah could work on it in the afternoons while Kitty rested and listened to her *Adventures in Odyssey* tapes.

Last she pulled out the new handmade journal she'd bought for herself. The stationary at Safe Anchorage was two or three times as expensive as what she could have found at Walmart. Trying not to feel guilty for her extravagance, she ran her fingers over the binding. Wondered what she should write about first.

It was always intimidating starting a new journal. So much pressure to make everything perfect from the start. It was a relief each time she made her first mistake or two and realized that her journal was far more gracious and forgiving than she was toward herself.

194

She picked up a pen from her nightstand and thought about what she should say.

Dear God ...

It was a good start, but then what? So many of her prayers lately — and nearly all the ones in her last journal — were about Scott. Even with those that started off as prayers for the unreached peoples of the world or conversations about how much she missed her mom, inevitably, after a paragraph, half a page at most, the subject always turned back to him.

She was ready for a change. She was tired of the sacrificial gift always getting off the altar, tired of daily surrendering her relationship with Scott to the Lord. It couldn't go on. It wasn't healthy for her, and it wasn't fair to Kitty either. This would be their first Christmas without their mom. Kitty needed a sister who was fully present, who was joyful and content, not a sister whose mind was on the other side of the country conjuring up dreams that could never come true.

Susannah knew how to start her journal.

There's something I need to get off my chest. I know that nothing comes as a surprise to you, Lord. Before a word is in my mouth you know it completely. Nothing is hidden from your sight, none of my thoughts or complaints or foolish longings.

God, you know how much time I've wasted over the past few months pining away for things that can never be. I don't want to live like that anymore. Just like Paul did, help me to forget the things that are behind and strain for what is ahead. I know you have a good future for me. I know all your plans for me are good, but I can't enjoy any of them when I'm still moping about the past.

Last year, you brought a wonderful, godly man into my life. As our relationship started to progress, I hoped that maybe it would turn into something deeper, but you have other plans for me. And I want to trust you, but I can't stop thinking about that Bible verse in Psalms about your perfect restoration. I can't stop thinking about Grandma Lucy's prayer on Sunday about how you carry everything you start to completion. Or her conversation tonight when she prayed for me and told me that you are the God who restores all things.

I've asked you so many times to take that hope and that dream away from me if it wasn't part of your plan, but now more than ever I'm asking you to somehow restore what was lost. Restore my relationship with Scott so that one day we can …

Susannah tore the page out of her journal and crumbled it up. Even when she tried to surrender her relationship with Scott to the Lord her unruly heart got in the way.

She put down her pen. There would be time for writing in the days to come. She'd try another prayer of surrender when she wasn't so tired. Now her only hope was that God would forgive her for clinging so tightly to dreams that could never come true and that her sleep would give her a few hours' reprieve from the restless longing in her soul.

CHAPTER 48

The phone rang while Susannah was looking for clean clothes for Kitty.

"Hello?" Why did her heart always skip that little beat whenever someone called?

"Susannah? That you?"

She didn't need caller ID to recognize the voice. "Hi, Ricky. Merry Christmas."

"Yeah, you too. We missed you at the Christmas Eve service tonight. Couldn't make it, huh?"

Susannah propped the phone against her shoulder and tried to get Kitty's things organized on her bed. "Yeah, it's pretty icy, and we don't want Kitty in big crowds where she can catch a cold or anything."

There she went using *we* as if she and Mom were both still around, both still making decisions about her sister's care.

"That makes sense. Well, I just wanted to say we missed you."

ALANA TERRY

Susannah wondered which *we* Ricky was referring to. Him and his mom?

"That's sweet of you to say."

"Hey, I know it's last minute." He cleared his throat. "And maybe you already have plans, but Mom says we've got plenty of food for tomorrow, and we could come pick you up so you don't have to worry about getting Kitty in the car by yourself. You know, if you wanted to come over for Christmas dinner. We could bring the truck and put her wheelchair in the back."

Susannah had the feeling she'd appreciate the thoughtful offer more if she didn't have two dozen different things to take care of at once.

"That's really nice of you to ask. It sounds fun, but ..."

"It's not a big group," he interrupted, "and Mom already checked. Nobody has a cold or anything, so you don't have to worry about germs."

Susannah sighed. "I'm sorry, we kind of already have plans. Nothing big, it's just Derek is coming over, and he's bringing a ham, so I think we'll just have a quiet day here."

"Oh. Ok."

She hated to think of disappointing him. "But I'll tell Kitty you invited her. It'll make her really happy to know you were thinking of her."

199

WHAT DREAMS MAY COME

"Uh-huh. Sure." Ricky's voice fell lifeless.

"Thanks again." Susannah did her best to infuse extra enthusiasm into her tone. "That's probably the nicest invitation I've gotten in quite a while."

She didn't mention it was also the only invitation.

She could hear his smile on the other end of the line. "Well, Mom says if tomorrow doesn't work out, maybe we'll plan on something else another time. After the holidays."

"Yeah," Susannah repeated mindlessly while she grabbed a clean chux pad to place on her sister's bed. "Sounds great."

She hung up the phone, realized the nightgown she'd planned to dress Kitty in was already soiled. She had meant to wash those clothes today. Finding nothing else clean, she decided her sister would be comfortable enough sleeping in her sweats and tossed the dirty nightgown into the pile of laundry that was now almost as high as her waist. She'd have to spend tomorrow cleaning before Derek came over for Christmas dinner.

The most wonderful time of the year, right?

Of course right.

CHAPTER 49

On Christmas morning. Susannah woke up early and blasted her mom's old CD recording of Handel's *Messiah*, which was as much of a cornerstone of a traditional Peters Christmas as Amish friendship bread at breakfast. Thankfully, Connie's starter from Safe Anchorage worked perfectly, and based on the sweet, yeasty smell from the oven, Susannah hadn't botched the recipe too terribly. As soon as she pulled the loaf out to cool, she hurried into Kitty's room. "Merry Christmas, sunshine."

Susannah was thankful for an extra dose of energy this morning. She'd thrown the friendship bread into the oven and still found time to make some muffins and start a much-needed load of laundry.

All month, Susannah had worried that Christmas would feel empty and pointless without her mother, but she'd woken up with more joy and excitement in her soul than she'd experienced in weeks. Maybe there was a real reason behind calling this a magical holiday.

God, thank you so much for sending Jesus down to earth to show us how to live and to pave the way for a relationship with you. Help today to be perfect, a day that would make Mom proud.

With that, she flipped on Kitty's light. "I said, 'Merry Christmas,'" she called out and started massaging her sister's back before she knew if she was even awake.

Twenty minutes later, Kitty was dressed and in her wheelchair at the dining room table, kicking her leg in approval while Susannah cut her first slice of friendship bread and let a dollop of butter melt on top of her cranberry muffin.

"Looks good," she told Kitty. "And what about you? You want vanilla or strawberry for your Christmas morning breakfast?"

Kitty nodded at the table and grunted.

"You want the friendship bread?" Susannah laughed. "How about I just put an extra teaspoon of sugar in your formula and we call it a deal?" She'd been joking, but Kitty reacted so enthusiastically Susannah hesitated and finally decided it couldn't do much harm.

Hopefully.

While her sister giggled like a little girl about to be caught sneaking a secular music tape into her home,

Susannah measured out half a teaspoon of sugar. "You sure you can afford all these extra calories?" she teased.

A grunt.

"Ok. It's your decision, not mine."

Snort.

Susannah laughed too as she dumped the sugar into her sister's bottle of formula. "Are you going to shake it up or should I?"

Blink.

"All right, but you better not tell anybody. It's got to stay our little secret. Deal?"

Blink.

Susannah helped her sister take her first sip of sweetened strawberry formula. Kitty was laughing so hard it would have taken a Christmas miracle if any actually found its way to her stomach, but for once Susannah wasn't going to let her sister's eating habits stress her out.

She wiped Kitty's chin with a napkin then impulsively leaned over and kissed her on the cheek. "Have I ever told you that you're the best sister in the world? Merry Christmas."

CHAPTER 50

Derek showed up fifteen minutes early with a ham warmed and glazed and ready to slice. Unfortunately, Susannah's afternoon cooking endeavors hadn't gone nearly as smoothly as that morning's. Whether from that tiny bit of extra sugar, the excitement of the day, or some random fluke, Kitty's digestion was all over that morning (literally), and by the time Susannah got her, the bathroom, and the bed completely cleaned up, it was time to put the green bean casserole in the oven. The only problem was she hadn't set foot in the kitchen since breakfast.

Derek didn't seem to mind the wait, and he sat with Kitty listening to *Adventures in Odyssey* while Susannah scurried around trying to prepare a few simple dishes.

I wonder, Lord, if you're giving me a little bit of a taste of how Martha felt when you were visiting her home.

At least Kitty had been in a good mood, explosive diarrhea and all. And her Christmas cheer was catching.

Thank you, God, for helping today go so much smoother

than it might have.

What she wanted to say was *thank you that I've been too busy to miss Mom very much*, but the confession made her feel guilty, so she focused on her green bean casserole, cornbread, and apple pie. A simple spread, especially compared to the meals her mom liked to prepare for holidays, but Derek wasn't expecting much, Kitty couldn't eat any of it anyway, and Susannah was too busy to even think about her own appetite.

At least she'd get some good sleep tonight. If Kitty's gut issues resolved by then.

But she wouldn't think about that. Christmas was the one day where she refused to let any anxious thoughts creep into her head. No maudlin moping around thinking about how nice it would be if Mom were in the kitchen working and Susannah were the one listening to *Odyssey* episodes. No pining away for the mission field or some passionate, godly missionary on the other side of the country.

Today was about keeping Kitty happy.

And making it through dinner without breaking down into tears.

That's why she stayed so busy. And eventually, all her hard work paid off. Dinner was nearly an hour late. She and Derek had to microwave the ham slices by the time all the other dishes were hot, but at quarter to five, the sparkling cider was poured and the plates were served.

Kitty pouted when Susannah refused to add an extra spoonful of sugar into her formula again, but otherwise everyone was in good spirits. Susannah wondered if Derek and she were both in the same awkward position, trying hard for Kitty's sake to keep a positive attitude when their hearts were empty and aching.

She and Derek might grow closer over the years, if he'd stick around long enough for her to get completely comfortable with him. Maybe. Only time would tell. Having him around, seeing the way he joked with her sister, reminded Susannah of how much energy it took just to keep Kitty engaged. It was so easy to make her laugh, but she was so compliant and easy-going that she was unfortunately easy to ignore too. Mom had been so good at talking to her throughout the day, asking her questions, and waiting politely for an answer. Susannah tried, but sometimes it sapped all her strength just to feed and bathe her sister so there wasn't any energy left for chit-chat.

After dinner, Derek cleared the table off while Susannah settled Kitty in her bed. "Are you ready to open some presents?" she asked.

Kick. Kick.

"Well, we have to wait for Derek to join us. Don't want him to be left out, do we?"

Kick.

When everything was ready, Kitty opened her gifts first.

"I'm going to make you a blanket," Susannah explained after helping Kitty tear off the wrapping paper. "I got the yarn from Safe Anchorage Farm. Isn't it pretty? Remember when Mom took us to see the goats they have there? Remember the cute little babies jumping all around?"

Kick. Kick.

"And here's my present for you." Derek reached over and pulled the colorful paper off a small rectangular box he placed in Kitty's hands.

"What is it?" Susannah asked.

"An MP3 player." He pointed to the box to show Kitty. "And it's got over five hundred *Adventures in Odyssey* episodes downloaded on it. All brand new."

"Five hundred?" Susannah repeated.

Kick, kick, kick, kick, kick.

Derek opened his travel mug next, and Susannah was a little embarrassed she'd given him something so generic. But he smiled and hugged her and froze in goofy poses with his gift to make Kitty laugh.

"And now." His expression suddenly got serious. He

WHAT DREAMS MAY COME

cleared his throat and looked at Susannah. "I asked Kitty the other night what she thought we should get you, and we came up with something together."

He reached into his back pocket and pulled out an envelope.

"This is from all of us."

At first, Susannah was afraid it would be full of cash. How did he expect her to accept a gift like that?

"Take a look," he urged.

Even Kitty was calm while Susannah opened it up.

"A plane ticket?"

"Read this first." Derek pointed to a brochure.

"The Urbana World Missions Conference?"

"It's a get-together for young adults and college students who are interested in Christian missions. They have all kinds of speakers. From the minute I heard about it, I knew it'd be perfect for you. And I knew you'd never agree to go unless I made you, so I already booked your spot at the conference, your room, your flight there, everything. You leave in two days."

"That soon?"

"They always have it right before New Year's. Now don't argue with me." His voice was firm. "Kitty wants you to go too, don't you?"

Blink.

A very tenuous blink.

"How can I … How will …"

"I'm taking vacation time. I'll stay here with Kitty. And Mrs. Fields and her son have agreed to come over and help too. We all know how Kitty feels about Ricky Fields, don't we?"

A cautious kick.

Derek nodded at the ticket in her hand. "It will be fine. I want you to go. It's something your mom and I were already planning to send you to this year. She's the one who first told me about it."

"Mom wanted me to go?"

He nodded. "She'd been talking about it for months."

"I don't know …" She looked at her sister.

"Your mom wanted it," he whispered again.

Susannah was beaten. "All right." She glanced again at the brochure, at the smiling faces on the cover. "I'll go."

CHAPTER 51

Susannah had never been around so many people her own age before. She forgot exactly how many Christians were in attendance. Twenty thousand? They were all over the place, spread out over the campus, flowing in all directions at once. Was this what it would be like to attend a big college?

The entire first day was a blur, from the early morning drive to the Spokane airport to the crammed shuttle to the university campus, not to mention the check-in procedure at the conference that felt even more involved than airport security. She'd been so overwhelmed by the sheer number of people around her and the general noise that she couldn't remember what the opening speaker talked about.

Terrified that she'd lose her way between the big conference center, the cafeteria, and her assigned dorm, she resolved to spend the next morning walking the campus and trying to find her bearings.

Lord, I know you brought me here for a reason, but this is way more overwhelming than I would have ever expected.

Guide me, Father. One step at a time, please. I need you.

The main conference events included speakers and comedy sketches and drama teams and a worship band that made Susannah feel closer to heaven than she thought humanly possible. In between were breakout sessions with missionaries from all around the world. Susannah listened to an ethnomusicologist talk about helping Christians develop indigenous styles of worship and a panel of speakers giving reports and updates on the persecuted church.

In one of the campus's huge halls were hundreds of tables where students and interested individuals could meet up with representatives from missionary sending agencies. For the first time, Susannah was glad that her future was clearly laid out for her in Orchard Grove, or she would have been overwhelmed from the sheer number of options. As it was, she found the hall far too crowded and noisy and preferred to spend her time in the breakout sessions. She thought it was strange that more of the students here didn't attend the smaller meetings. Sometimes she was one of only two or three attendees, which fortunately gave her the chance to ask questions and feel like she'd gotten to know some of the missionaries personally.

Yes, Lord, Mom and Derek were right. This is so refreshing.

She'd taken her new journal with her, and when she wasn't in one of the breakout meetings or group sessions, she'd find her way to the room they'd set up as a prayer chapel and write. For the first time, she wasn't just scribbling about Scott.

Lord, you are so big. Your heart for the nations is even greater than I ever imagined. I realize now how lonely I've been in Orchard Grove. It's so inspiring to be here with other believers who want to take your gospel to the ends of the earth.

She didn't know how or why, but for the first time since her mom died, Susannah didn't feel trapped at the thought of spending the rest of her life in Orchard Grove. Nearly all of the missionaries she'd met in the breakout sessions talked about how important it was to have an intercession team back home, and Susannah realized that prayer wasn't just a last resort. It was the power through which the gospel was spread, missionaries were equipped, and God's glory was taken to the nations. She'd used all of the spending money Derek sent her with to buy prayer guides and other resources to take back with her to Orchard Grove. She even had a few audiobooks she could listen to that would guide her prayers for the nations and that she could listen to while she was cleaning or cooking or getting Kitty ready for the day.

She'd also been convicted here about how little time she spent each day helping Kitty grow in her spiritual walk. Kitty loved the Lord, would joyfully try to sing along with the hymns their mom played on the piano, but there was so much more Susannah could teach her. How to pray for different countries. How to intercede for missionaries. She was out of funds, but as soon as she got home, she wanted to find a map of the world and tape it up on Kitty's wall. She pictured them sitting in Kitty's room for an hour or two every day praying for God to send his workers to the different countries of the world.

Susannah couldn't go to the mission field, but that didn't mean God wouldn't use her to advance his kingdom worldwide. The best part of it was she never had to leave Orchard Grove. Unless it was to come back here. With careful budgeting, she could afford to come back next time. Receive that same excitement she now felt in her soul, the excitement she was eager to carry back with her to Orchard Grove.

Lord, thank you so much for putting this idea in Mom's head. Thank you for Derek remembering and forcing me to come here. Thank you for all the people here that you've called to spread your gospel around the world, and thank you for opening my eyes to the part I can play in spreading your kingdom like wildfire across the land.

She glanced at the clock on the wall of the prayer chapel

and closed her journal. The next breakout session was in five minutes. It was a talk she'd been looking forward to about creating a missions prayer program in your local church. Susannah had never considered herself a leader in any way, but she knew God was calling her to stay in Orchard Grove. Most people there never thought about the Great Commission beyond the annual December offering they collected to distribute to the few missionaries the church supported.

She was nervous about stepping up into a more active role in her church, but she also felt the weight of responsibility pressing down on her. God had given her a passion for world missions and yet kept her from ever leaving Orchard Grove. Instead of complaining about the way her life had turned out, she could spend her energy not only praying for the gospel to spread but encouraging others around her to do the same.

It wasn't hopping on a plane to take care of children at an orphanage in India or teach classes to kids in Africa, but it was the work God had called her to.

She didn't want to fail.

CHAPTER 52

Scott stared around the room. Empty. He should have known. Talking about ways that local believers could encourage their churches to become more missions oriented wasn't the kind of flashy or exciting topic that would draw in hundreds of attendees. Which is probably why his co-worker had pawned the responsibility off on him. Oh, well.

Scott always enjoyed the Urbana conference. He hadn't missed one since he'd started working for Kingdom Builders twelve years ago. There was something so invigorating about surrounding himself with young people who loved the Lord and wanted to serve him overseas.

Of course, not everybody who got excited here would end up on the mission field. He figured that even if a third of the attendees here made a commitment to pursue full-time ministry like the conference managers claimed, only a small fraction of those would actually turn into career missionaries. The distractions of the world were far too strong.

For years, Scott had looked down on those who graduated with him from Bible college, those who'd planned to serve God vocationally but ended up doing something else. Now, he had a deeper understanding of the ways God worked and knew a Christian could be involved in full-time ministry while still working a secular job. The fact that the world needed Christian missionaries didn't negate the fact that it also needed Christian doctors and teachers and journalists and janitors and taxicab drivers.

So he had learned to stop judging others, but he did sometimes wonder what would happen if God called a Christian to a specific mission field and the believer didn't follow through. Would God just raise somebody else up to minister in that region? If God was going to save everyone that he wanted to save as some Christians believed, if a Christian could ignore God's call to the mission field and rest assured that the Lord would just invite somebody more willing, where was the sense of urgency? Why would he ask young people to sacrifice their futures, their comforts, their worldly dreams if eternal souls weren't at risk of perishing without hearing the gospel message?

These were questions better fit for the four corners of his alma mater, but he still confronted them on occasion. Once, when he was speaking at a church just outside of

Philadelphia to raise support for Kingdom Builders, an old man had asked him why he bothered traveling across the world with the gospel when there were so many hurting and needy people right in his own backyard.

Those kinds of confrontations always bothered him, reminding him of the way Hudson Taylor was discouraged from preaching the gospel in China because "when God pleases to convert the heathen, he'll do it without the help of people like you and me." Scott was in full support of local missions, but how could that be an excuse to ignore those in other parts of the world who had never even had the chance to hear the gospel of Jesus Christ?

He glanced again at the time. If nobody showed up in the next few minutes, he would probably call the session off.

A timid knock sounded on the door, and he hoped that whoever came to hear what he had to say brought a few friends along. There was nothing more awkward than standing in front of the room giving a speech meant for twenty or thirty people to an audience of one.

"Come in," he called out without raising his eyes.

The little startled sound that followed made him look up.

"Am I in the right place?"

He would recognize that sound anywhere. He could have been riding in a crowded Moscow subway surrounded by two dozen sweaty Russian men, and he still would have known that voice.

He licked his lips, suddenly aware that he was dizzy. Did she recognize him too? Is that why she had gasped when she stepped through the doorway?

He was on his feet. Ignoring the way the room spun in circles around him. Watching her face to tell if she was happy to see him or not.

Maybe he was wrong. What would she be doing all the way out here? What about her sister?

That must be it. After he'd tried so hard to get her out of his head, after he'd prayed so fervently for God to help him get over the pain of losing her, his mind was playing tricks. There were twenty thousand people at this conference. How many of them would be young women with golden, flowing hair and large, trusting eyes?

Eyes that probed into his very soul.

He cleared his throat, reminding himself that he had a presentation to deliver. Convincing himself that Susannah Peters was back home with her sister in Orchard Grove.

"Are you here for the talk on starting a missions movement in your local church?" he asked.

Why was she staring at him like that? Why wouldn't she sit down?

"Make yourself comfortable." He pointed to one of the desks, but she didn't move. She looked just like he imagined her all these months. The resemblance was uncanny. "What's your name? Where are you from?"

She blinked up at him. Those large trusting eyes. "I'm Susannah. Have we met before?"

CHAPTER 53

She wasn't sure whether to laugh or cry or run away.

"Susannah? You're Susannah?"

When she first stepped into the room, she'd convinced herself she was imagining things. Sure, the man in front of her looked like Scott, but the name of the presenter was listed as something else.

She'd thought he'd acted a little odd when she entered, but there were all kinds of possible explanations for that. Even after she heard his voice, that same voice that had been in her mind for months, she told herself it was just a coincidence. He stared at her like he thought he knew her, but that could be easily explained. She did have a fairly generic face and common features.

It wasn't until she saw his reaction when she told him her name that she knew.

He stood staring at her with a smile half formed on his face as if he couldn't decide on the appropriate expression and gave up trying. "It's me. It's Scott."

She should go. This was a test. That's all it was. God had asked her to give up her dreams of the future with him, and now he was allowing the devil to tempt her one more time. All she had to do was pass this test, and she could be over him forever.

Except her feet refused to move. She tried to snap her brain to attention, tried to force herself to say something intelligible, but all that came out was, "Scott?"

He laughed. "Yeah, it's me."

She could tell he was nervous. Uncertain. So was she. He was bigger than she'd expected. Taller. She'd seen his picture on the Kingdom Builders webpage, but he looked older than she'd pictured. She felt like a child staring up at him.

"What are you doing here?"

"How long have you been here?"

They spoke at the same time. Both questions had obvious answers.

He laughed again. This time, so did she. Cautiously. Remembering how painful it was to give him up before. Making sure she'd never have to live through that kind of agony again.

Sacrificing someone like him once was enough.

"Do you want to sit down?" He pulled out a chair. "Or

maybe we could go on a walk. I'm scheduled to give a lecture here, but it doesn't seem like anyone else is coming."

Susannah's throat had never felt so dry before. "It was somebody else's name on the list." She had to almost squeak the words out.

"Yeah, Buck got pulled to talk on a panel, so I told him I'd take over here. But wait a minute, are you telling me you've been here at the conference this whole time?"

She nodded, still wondering what she was supposed to do. Should she run away and hide? It wasn't right for God to drag her through four agonizing months of trying to give Scott up to him and then to dangle him in front of her face like a box of forbidden pastries.

God, what are you doing?

Her mind went back to the morning just a few days before Christmas when she'd read through Psalm 85. Then to her time in the back room at the Safe Anchorage gift shop, when Grandma Lucy had prayed for God to restore all that she had lost.

Is that what this was? Could it be that God wasn't testing her resolve to get over Scott but that he was actually answering her prayers?

In her deepest thoughts and darkest musings, isn't this exactly what she had hoped for?

She didn't know what she hoped for. That was the problem. It was too much. Too confusing.

Scott was looking at her with worry in his eyes. "Are you all right? Is this too hard for you? Should I go?"

God, you need to show me what to do. You need to help me know what to say.

She opened her mouth. Fumbled over her words. Finally managed to croak, "No, you don't have to go anywhere."

CHAPTER 54

Scott still couldn't believe it. Couldn't believe she was actually here. Couldn't believe that in an hour when the conference hall closed, he was actually going to take her out to dinner before that night's general session. Their initial meeting was so painfully awkward he couldn't think about it without a sense of embarrassed regret.

Once they both got over the shock of running into each other, they had gone for a walk around the university campus. Scott had a whole hour and a half before he was due back at the Kingdom Builders booth in the conference hall, but it wasn't anywhere near enough time for him to catch up with Susannah and hear everything she'd gone through since they last talked.

Life had been hard on her. She'd tried to sugarcoat it, had presented it in the best light possible, but he knew her so well he could tell how burdened she was from taking care of Kitty, how heavy her spirit was from mourning her mother's death. Scott wanted to take her in his arms right then,

224

comfort her, tell her that she'd never have to be lonely again. Just say the word, and they could spend the rest of their lives together. But her sense of duty to her family had ripped her out of his life, and he wasn't about to scare her away again.

That's why he hadn't asked her to come back to the conference hall with him. If he had his choice, she'd stand by his side for the rest of the afternoon. He didn't want to take his eyes off her, didn't want to risk losing her. Not again. Now that he'd seen her, now that they'd spent an hour and a half not just talking but actually in the same location, the same time zone, having a face-to-face conversation for the very first time, he realized more than ever how empty the past four months had been without her.

How bleak the future looked if she wasn't in it.

It would take time. That's what he kept telling himself over and over. Time to earn her trust. Susannah was timid. He could tell just from her body language, the way she hugged her arms against herself as they walked through the crowded building, how out of place she felt here. Had she ever seen a crowd this large before? She was scared. Overwhelmed, and if she felt anything like he did, she was terrified that their walk together this afternoon had been some sort of dream. A delusion.

Patience. That's what he needed. But all he wanted to do

was hold her close against his chest and tell her how much he loved her. How he had loved her before he'd even met her in person. How he wanted nothing more than for them to spend the rest of their lives together.

He was already working out his plans. How he could transfer his work to Washington and telecommute from Orchard Grove. He'd tell his missions director that he could only travel abroad once a year. Twice at most. Any fears he'd previously entertained about feeling trapped in the States paled next to the thought of losing Susannah again.

He would love Kitty. He would be the most devoted brother-in-law the world had known.

No, he was getting ahead of himself. That was the kind of impulsive thinking that would scare Susannah away. He would wait. Wait for God's timing. And until then praise the Lord for bringing such a godly woman back into his life.

CHAPTER 55

"Where are we going?" Susannah asked.

"A few of my buddies and I found a nice burrito place. It's not far, only about a ten-minute walk. You aren't too cold, are you?"

Susannah didn't tell him that she could brave Siberian winter as long as he stood confidently by her side.

That afternoon, after they'd taken a walk together and he returned to the Kingdom Builders booth in the conference hall, it took every ounce of self-control in Susannah's spirit not to follow him there. She didn't know what she would do, maybe just sit behind him and let the realization that he was actually here sink in.

Instead, she had returned to the prayer chapel and poured her heart out to the Lord in her journal.

God, the last thing I want to do is make you disappointed in me again by letting someone come between me and your plans for my life. I'm so confused right now. Part of me is afraid that Scott's going to want to talk about our relationship again, only I have no idea what to tell him. The rest of me is terrified we'll just spend these last two days of this conference together, then go our own ways, and that will be it. I don't know how to go back to Orchard Grove now. I don't know what to expect. I've tried so hard to learn the secret to being content, to serve where you've called me, but now my mind is racing and my spirit is crying out for you to guide me.

Mom told me to protect my heart. I did a terrible job with that, and I've suffered the consequences ever since she died. Now she's not here to give me warnings, to tell me what to do. So I have to trust you. You know that if I spend any more time with Scott, it's going to be nearly impossible for me to not fall in love with him again. Now that we've been together, I realize there was never a time when I stopped loving him. I just denied those emotions because I thought that's what you wanted me to do.

And now he's here, and it's even harder to protect my heart. I love him, Lord. I've loved him almost from the very beginning. And I did what I could to be the kind of wise, prudent girl Mom raised me to be, but I gave my heart to him so long ago, and the whole time we've gone without talking I've been missing him because I've been missing part of myself.

You are the God who restores, but you are also the God who takes away. You took my mother away, and she's someone I know I can never have back again on this side of heaven. And that pain is still so fresh. So raw. I'm scared that even if things start to go well again with Scott that you'll change your mind, that you'll rip him away from me a second time, and I'm so tired of mourning. I'm so tired of this heaviness that hangs over me, that steals the abundant joy you promised to those who put their trust in you.

I'm afraid to do it, God, but I'm going to put my hope in you again. Hope that you will guide me and that you'll understand it's too hard for me to protect my own heart. You'll have to do it for me. If Scott's not the one, if there isn't any future for the two of us together, if you led us to meet each other at this conference just so we could get some sense of closure, I need to you to make that so obvious to us both. Close those doors.

But if that's not the case, if you really do have a way in mind for Scott and me to pick up where we left off, to combine our commitment for you and our passion for missions and my love for my sister and make something actually work out of it, then and only then may things progress any farther than they already have.

I know I'm asking a lot of you, Lord, and I have no right to assume you'll listen to me, but I pray that out of your grace you'll either take Scott Phillips out of my life forever or you'll bring us together where we'll never have to say goodbye again.

Susannah thought over the words to her prayer as she and Scott made their way to the restaurant.

"You're quiet," he remarked once they were a block or two off campus.

"Just got distracted for a minute." She blushed, but he kept his eyes straight ahead and didn't seem to notice.

Lord, I wonder what he's thinking about.

Could it be all those late nights they'd spent talking about their heart for the nations, their plans for the future?

Could it be that ring he'd bought her and never had the opportunity to place on her finger?

No, she couldn't rush into things. *That's what I mean, God. I'm no good at guarding my own heart, so you've got to do it for me.*

When a strip of restaurants and store fronts came into view, Scott broke the strained silence. "What are you thinking about?"

Susannah scurried for a response. "Just wondering how Kitty's doing."

He smiled down at her. She would have never guessed it from his picture, but he was so tall she barely came up to the middle of his chest.

"It must be hard to be away from her so long when you love her that much." There was tenderness in his eyes. A significance to his words that she didn't want to acknowledge.

Her heart quickened, and before she realized it, they had stopped walking. Where was the restaurant? Why weren't they moving anymore?

He leaned forward.

Susannah's heart fluttered like the wings of a hummingbird. *Dear God, he's going to do something stupid. Please make him stop.*

He reached out his hand. Brushed a little strand of hair that the wind had whipped across her face.

It was the first time they touched.

He leaned down farther.

No, Lord. This is too soon. Tell him to back away.

"Susannah Peters?" The words reverberated throughout her entire body even though he was whispering.

She looked up, her voice quivering. Her whole body quivering. "Yes?"

The smile he rained down on her sent a flood of heat and comfort through her being.

"I'm really glad I found you."

CHAPTER 56

Scott had spent nearly the past year wondering what it would be like to sit across from Susannah at a restaurant and watch her eat.

Now, after months of impatient waiting and painful separation, he finally knew. She had a little dimple in her cheek. He had noticed it in her senior picture but couldn't have guessed the way it became more pronounced when she chewed. Her hair was even softer than he'd imagined. It took all his self-possession not to reach out and stroke it.

He was lost in her eyes, the gentle beauty that flowed from her expression, the tenderness that graced every move she made.

She caught him staring and paused with her fork in the air. "What do you keep looking at?"

"You."

She blushed deeply, and he loved her for it.

"I could watch you eat every day of my life." He hadn't meant to say it that way. He was just trying to be honest. "I

232

mean ..." He started to stammer an apology but gave up and finally just said, "It's really nice having you here."

She smiled softly. "I know what you mean."

Her words emboldened him. He knew he was about to make a fool of himself, but he couldn't help it. "Susannah?"

"Yes?" Her eyes were so wide. So full of love. Not the romantic, passionate love he bore in his heart for her. Pure, selfless love. The kind of love that allowed her to put her life permanently on hold to care for her sister. The kind of love that sustained her through her mother's death, keeping her sensitive and gentle in spite of all the grief she'd suffered.

He cleared his throat, clutched his Diet Coke as if it might give him strength, and said, "There's something I need to tell you."

He paused, half expecting her to stop him. Half expecting her to protest that it was too much, too soon.

She remained quiet. Waiting with that soft, quiet expression.

"It's about us. About you and me."

Her lip quivered once, but her voice was steady when she said, "Ok."

Now that he'd started, he wasn't sure he could finish. He took a gulp of soda. Anything to steady his nerves. "Well, months ago, almost a year now, I asked you to start praying about our relationship. You remember that?"

"I remember." Her eyes were still so full, so trusting, but now he thought a glimpse of something else too. Hope?

"And I told you that I was going to pray about it too. See if maybe God had plans for us to deepen our relationship, if maybe it might lead to … if over time it might slowly develop into something more."

She nodded. It was all the encouragement he needed.

"I've never stopped thinking about you." The words poured out of him now, like water spilling over a dam. "You were right when you told me we had to call it off. As hard as it was, I realize that was a step you had to take, a sacrifice you had to make. You've done so much for your sister, and I can only imagine how much grace and love and strength it takes to do what you do. And maybe you think that nobody sees you. That God's just left you there to take care of Kitty for the rest of your life, and you'll never get noticed or thanked or appreciated for it. But you're wrong. No, don't interrupt me. I know you don't do it for the applause or the recognition. That's just what makes you who you are. It's what makes me …"

He stopped himself short.

"It's what makes me admire you so much. But it's more than that."

He leaned forward. Was there any way to make her understand? Open up his heart and show her the love he had for her? Did she realize? Could she ever guess?

"I've loved you since the first day we talked on that phone. Maybe now's not the best time to admit something like this, but I can't help it. I've spent the past four months without you, wondering what might have happened between us, and I know that if I don't tell you everything that's on my heart right now, I'll never be able to forgive myself.

"I love you. I've never stopped loving you. When I think about the future, when I pray about God's plans for me, everything feels dark unless I'm thinking about you. A few months after we met, I asked you to pray about our relationship, to start asking God if it's meant to progress beyond friendship or romance, and I told you that I'd be praying too. Well, I've prayed. For the past half a year or more I've hardly prayed about anything else. And every time I told God that I was going to give you up, every time I asked him to help me take you out of my heart, you came back again. And now you're here, and we're together. Neither of us planned it this way. We could have gone the entire conference without ever bumping into each other, but God led us together."

His heart was pounding. He wondered if Susannah could hear it from her seat.

"I know it wasn't a mistake. I know it wasn't an accident. And I know at first you said we couldn't be together because you had a duty to take care of your sister and I had a call to serve God as a missionary. But being a missionary is more than where you live. It's more than how much you travel. You felt years ago that God called you to be a missionary, and now you're confused because you can't leave Orchard Grove. But you don't see what I see. I see a woman who spent a year working at an assisted living home, praying with the sick and the elderly, spreading the gospel there. You remember that man you baptized in the shower because he'd asked Jesus into his heart and his family didn't want the chaplain to visit? Or your co-worker, Tiff, the one you kept telling me was so hardened by life but who's now saved? God's been using you as a missionary for years, and you don't even know it.

"I wish I could give you my eyes so you could see what I see when I look at you. You are the most compassionate, gentle-spirited person I know, and I've met all kinds of believers over the years all across the globe. But there's none as sweet or as giving or as selfless as you, and there's none I would rather spend the rest of my life with."

After he got this part out, he dared to glance up. It wasn't the tears streaking down Susannah's cheeks that he first noticed or way her lips trembled.

It was the love and joy that was shining in her eyes, the love and joy that answered his question before he found the courage to ask.

Slipping onto his knee, he took her hand in his. "I can't show you any ring because I left it back in Massachusetts, so you'll have to use your imagination. Susannah Wesley Peters, will you be my wife?"

CHAPTER 57

She said yes. The entire time he was talking, from the moment she suspected the question that might be coming, she'd planned on telling him something different. *Wait.* Or *you should ask my stepdad.* Or *I need to pray about it first.*

Instead, she'd opened her mouth and said *yes.* Ignoring the small applause from the few other diners in the restaurant who'd watched the intensely personal exchange, she threw her arms around his neck and repeated that small, beautiful word.

"Yes."

He stood and wrapped her arm around his waist, swinging her in a circle. "Really?" He let out a full belly laugh. A glorious sound. "You mean it? You're saying yes?"

She laughed again while tears of both bittersweet sorrow and joy mingled down her cheeks. "Yes," she repeated. She'd say it a hundred times if she had to. The word itself felt so freeing, so powerful.

He kissed her cheek, his scruffy stubble scratching her skin. "I can do that now because we're engaged, can't I?"

She still hadn't stopped laughing. Hadn't stopped saying that magnificent word. "Yes."

He kissed her again, this time on the corner of her mouth.

"And that one was ok, too?"

"Yes." *A hundred times, yes.*

"Well now, what about this?"

When she'd thought about kissing someone for the first time, she'd been afraid she'd have no idea what to do, but this kiss was fresh and pure and tender.

She wanted more.

But he put her down, collapsing breathless into his seat. "You've just made me the happiest man in the world. You know that, don't you?"

Susannah looked around her as if for the first time. A painted picture of a bullfighter hung just to the right of Scott's shoulder. On the other side of him was a still-life vase full of flowers. So many colors. So much life.

So much joy.

He took both her hands in his, but all she could think about was that last kiss.

"It's getting late," he told her. "We should probably start walking back if we're going to get to the general session on time."

His voice sounded as if it were traveling through water.

Her pulse surged through her ears. She'd never known you could actually hear your own heartbeat that loud and clear.

He glanced at her half-eaten burrito. "Do you want to pack that up and save it for later?"

Food? How could he think about eating at a time like this?

What was supposed to happen next? Would they hold hands like this for the rest of the night? Would he kiss her again before they got back to campus? Would he sit through the general session with his arm wrapped around her waist?

What would Kitty think when she came home and told her sister she was engaged? What would the people at Orchard Grove say? Would they gossip about her for daring to find joy after her mother's death? Would Derek understand, or would he regret sending her off to the conference?

And in the end, did it really matter? She had prayed for this for months. Even those times when she was trying to voice a prayer of surrender, in her heart, this is exactly what she'd been asking God for.

And he answered.

Gloriously, powerfully, miraculously, he answered.

Susannah didn't know what would happen next. Would they have a short engagement like her mom and Derek?

Would they be separated again for months before Scott could make it out to Orchard Grove? Would they move right into her mom's house or look for a place of their own with more room for Kitty? Would he keep on traveling with Kingdom Builders? Would she ever find the opportunity to go on mission trips with him?

She didn't know the answers to any of those questions. All she knew was that God had peered into her heart, understood her most secret desires, the ones she didn't even dare wish for, and he'd poured out more blessings on her than she have imagined.

As she and Scott walked side by side into the dusk on their way to worship God with twenty thousand other believers, Grandma Lucy's words played through Susannah's mind.

The Lord is faithful, and he who began a good work in you will carry it on to completion.

'Do I bring to the moment of birth and not give delivery?' says the LORD. 'Do I close up the womb when I bring to delivery?' says your God.

Joy swelled up in her heart. She was glad that the general sessions always started with a time of worship and singing or else she was certain her spirit couldn't contain all the gratitude and praises ready to pour out of her.

You've seen the sacrifices she's made, and in your good plans you will restore all that was once lost.

God had done that and infinitely more. It didn't matter that the future was still uncertain. It didn't matter that she had questions about how she and Scott could care for Kitty and continue serving God with the Kingdom Builders.

All that mattered was God had seen her in her deepest sorrow, and in the soil of her grief had planted seeds that now sprouted and bloomed into the most beautiful, glorious harvest of joy she could have dared hope for.

She stopped walking. Looked up at Scott with a heart bursting from happiness.

"What is it?" he asked, matching her grin.

She realized he was too tall. Even on tiptoes, she couldn't reach him unless he bent down. "Come here." She wrapped her arms around his neck. Pulled his face down toward her.

"I've always loved you," she whispered the moment right before her lips melted into his.

And she would continue to love him for as long as they both should live.

A NOTE FROM THE AUTHOR

What Dreams May Come is based off the true story of my courtship with my husband. I met Scott in 2002 when I emailed a missionary agency and asked for information about their summer internship program in Siberia. Scott, who had recently returned from a short-term trip to that region, was my "recruiter." We progressed from emails to a phone interview where Scott determined if I would be a good fit for the missions team. Just a few weeks later we were spending nearly all our free time on the phone with one another. I was a college student near Boston at the time, and he was working in LA. I do not have a sister with disabilities, but there were other issues that for a while made it look like Scott and I could never end up together, and we broke up for four months (even though at the time we still hadn't seen each other face to face). In spite of the distance, time zone differences, and many other obstacles stacked against us, we finally met at the Urbana World Missions Conference where Scott was a presenter for his missionary agency and I was a student participant. He proposed at the conference, and we were married six months later.

It was always my dream to write out our story, and even though *What Dreams May Come* is a fictionalized version, I'm thankful for the chance to put our history on paper. This project was kept a secret from Scott until he opened the paperback version on Christmas morning. And since I know he's reading this, *Surprise! I love you so much. Who would have imagined that in spite of all the obstacles we faced as a young couple that God would bring us together and sustain our relationship to where we are now? You are my living proof that dreams come true and that God is able to do infinitely and immeasurably more than all we could ask or imagine.*

32744879R00151

Made in the USA
Middletown, DE
08 January 2019